The Devil's Breath

Dahn Alexander Batchelor

iUniverse, Inc.
Bloomington

This is a work of fiction. All of the characters, names, incidents, organizations, and dialogue in this novel are either the products of the author's imagination or are used fictitiously.

iUniverse books may be ordered through booksellers or by contacting:

iUniverse
1663 Liberty Drive
Bloomington, IN 47403
www.iuniverse.com
1-800-Authors (1-800-288-4677)

ISBN: 978-1-4502-8350-2 (sc)
ISBN: 978-1-4502-8353-3 (hc)
ISBN: 978-1-4502-8352-6 (e)

Printed in the United States of America

iUniverse rev. date: 1/30/2012

Chapter One

Andre Verlain, a 26-year-old doctor living in Paris was excited that he had been invited to spend a week at the chateau of Vicomte du Marcel Valmonte of Sarthe during the third week of March 1902. It was actually the Vicomte's son, Henri who had invited him since he too, like Andre was a doctor at the Saint-Antoine University Hospital in Paris. He and Andre were close friends and had been for several years. The chateau was larger than most buildings in Paris and unlike most buildings in the beautiful City of Lights, the furnishings in the chateau were exquisitely created. The grounds were as magnificent as he had ever seen as they extended all the way to the banks of the River des Veigers which in itself was a beautiful winding river southwest of city of Le Mans, a small city that is southwest of Paris.

But what really excited him was that during the week he was at the chateau, the five guests were going to be entertained by the famous soothsayer, Madam Boulier who was renowned for forecasting events in the future. In fact, she was the soothsayer who forecasted that on March 9th 1902, the famous symphony composer, Gustav Mahler would marry Alma Schindler in Vienna and on the next day, an earthquake would destroy the Turkish city of Tocjangri; events that actually occurred on the days she had forecasted.

After a sumptuous supper, the five guests and their host along with Madam Boulier entered a salon in which a round table had been placed in the center of the small room with seven chairs surrounding it. As everyone sat down around the table, the lights were turned down by the butler until only the undefined images of the seven people sitting around the table could be seen against the backdrop of the dimly-lit walls. The soothsayer, a woman who appeared to be in her seventies, then placed a short stubby candle in the centre of the table and had the butler light it for her. Now everyone could see the faces of everyone else sitting around the table. All of them except Madam Boulier fixed their eyes on the flame as they listened to her voice.

Andrew fidgeted as he listened to Madam Boulier forecast the futures of the five people ahead of him. The man, whose future was being forecasted for him immediately before his own, said to the soothsayer, "I am going to St. Petersburg to see that magnificent city." Then he asked, "Will I meet a beautiful woman in that city?"

The soothsayer looked up at the young man and said, "Do not go near the Marie Palace on April second."

"Why not?" he asked and then he immediately followed it up with a statement. "That is one of the really beautiful palaces in that city. Why should I miss the opportunity to see it?"

The soothsayer paused for a moment and then replied, "Someone on that day will be murdered in that palace."

One of the other guests asked, "Who will it be?"

The soothsayer replied, "I do not know but I do know that someone is going to be murdered that day in that palace."

She then turned to Andre and asked, "Do you have a question for me, young man?"

Andrew thought for a brief moment and then said, "I am going to the city of St. Pierre on the island of Martinique to marry the woman I truly love." He paused for a moment and then asked, "Will I marry her?"

The soothsayer didn't say a word for two minutes and then she said, "The woman you will truly be in love with will not marry you."

"But," exclaimed Andre, "She and her parents promised me that we can be married when I arrive on the island."

As Andrew look at the light from the candle flickering in the soothsayer's eyes while waiting for a reply, she finally spoke and said with sadness in her voice, "The woman you will desire to marry will be doomed as will everyone else in the city of St. Pierre. Only one will survive and it will not be the one you will truly love."

Andre was aghast. He tried to think of another question but he couldn't. Despite his concern, he was determined to sail to the island in any case even though he later learned that on April 2nd, Dmitry Sipyagin, the Minister of Interior of the Russian Empire, was assassinated by a terrorist in the Marie Palace in St Petersburg just as the soothsayer had forecasted.

Andre had been at sea for six long weary weeks on board the three-masted French barque, the *Mirabeau* that had left its home port, Roquefort, France, on April 8th 1902. The barque was 54 metres in length, 8.53 metres in width and its displacement was 513 tonnes. It was scheduled to arrive at its final destination by the first week of May. Martinique, as Andre had been told, was one of the most beautiful of all the islands of the Windward Islands in the Caribbean. Rising from the waterfront to the green hillsides that lead back toward the slopes of the volcano, Pelee was the small city of St. Pierre that was home to 27 thousand inhabitants. Being at sea on a square rigger, or for that matter on any sailing boat for any real length of time is not what the average traveler desired but nevertheless Andre had decided to take the trip because of his dream, that dream being; to be married to a beautiful girl who not only had beauty, but also wealth. The object of his love was Rachel Hayot, a twenty-year old girl who was the only child of a rich plantation owner whose plantation was just outside the city of St. Pierre. As the twenty-six-year-old stood on the deck watching the sea glide past the boat, his thoughts took him back to Paris the previous year where he was a young intern in one of Paris's finest and oldest hospitals.

Rachel had been in Paris with her parents for their annual vacation, and she had caught a bad case of influenza and was hospitalized for a month. It wasn't his intention to fall in love with this charming, beautiful girl from the colonies but somehow he found himself spending more attention to Rachelle then to the rest of his patients.

Rachel reciprocated the love and it was almost a sure thing that their plans to marry was in the offing but her parents squelched that as soon as they suspected that their relationship was obviously more than just that of doctor and patient. He would never forget the day she left the hospital with her parents. Her mother was very cold and aloof however her father had suggested that if Andre was willing to wait one year before deciding on marrying his daughter, he would be more receptive to Andre's proposal to his daughter after both of them had a chance to think it over.

A year had elapsed and Rachel's letters were very encouraging so Andre decided to go to Martinique, marry her and then take his wife back to France. Fortunately he had finished his internship at the hospital and after the hospital offered him a permanent post in the hospital; the administrators granted him leave of absence until the first of July. To arrive back in Paris meant that he had to leave the island on the *Rormania* on the eighth of May. The *Mirabeau* was due to arrive at Martinique by the first of the month and that meant he had seven full days to convince Rachel's parents of his love for their daughter.

"Verlain," a voice cried out in a distance. "Doctor Verlain!" the voice cried out again.

Andre turned away from the boat's railing and saw a seaman approaching him. "Sir." the seaman began. "The Captain says he would like you to meet with him up forward."

"Very well," answered Andre, "Lead me to him."

The two men walked the length of the boat and the seaman pointed to a hatchway.

"He's waiting for you down there, Sir." said the seaman as he turned away and headed back aft.

Andre climbed down the steps leading into the forecastle and was met by another seaman who then led him into a passageway and then through a series of hatchways. Finally they entered a small room and Andre came face to face with the captain. He was a man in his fifties and from what Andre had learned from some of the crew, he had been at sea since he first served as a cabin boy at the age of fourteen. He was partially bald but had a full beard.

"Thank you very much for coming, Doctor Verlain. I would appreciate it greatly if you would take a look at one of my men. He has been complaining of a pain in his belly."

Lying on one of the bunks was a man stripped to his waist.

"Tell me about the pain." asked Andre in a professional manner that he hoped would give some reassuring psychological relief to the seaman.

"Yes, Sir. I have had a pain on the right side of my stomach for the past few days."

"Have you been feeling nauseated?"

"Yes, Sir." replied the seaman as he winced.

Andre pressed gently on the man's lower abdomen then released the pressure suddenly. The man screamed in pain and clutched at his lower abdomen. Andre took the Captain by the arm and led him to the other end of the room.

"Well, Sir. It looks like he may have an inflamed appendix."

"Will you have to operate, Doctor?" asked the captain.

"I am not sure. How far are we from St. Pierre?"

"If the weather holds out, perhaps eight or nine hours. The island should not be too far over the horizon according to my reckoning."

"Well, Captain, I think that it might be better if we wait until we arrive at St. Pierre where he can get proper medical care."

Suddenly a scream came from the bunk and the two men hurried to the side of the seaman who was now squirming in pain on the bunk.

"I think eight or nine hours may be too late, Doctor."

"Well, Sir, I will operate if you wish but you must understand that I have never performed an operation such as this on my own. I only assisted once."

"The man will die if you don't operate, Doctor." He spoke with some authority on that subject having lost a man in a similar way several years earlier.

"I will ask the seaman if he is agreeable to me doing the operation and if he is, then I will perform it." said Andre.

Andre looked at the squirming man and then turned to the Captain again and asked, "What's his name?"

"Jacques."

Andre approached the seaman and spoke softly to him, Jacques. "Do you know what is wrong with you?"

"No, Sir. Perhaps I have eaten too much."

"Or drunk too much." added one of his shipmates with a smile.

"No, not much chance of that." replied the stricken man with an eye on his captain.

"Well, I will attempt to describe it to you. There is a finger-shaped sac three to six inches long which protrudes from your large bowel." Andre pointed to the lower right quarter of the man's abdomen, then he continued. "It is called an appendix and if it gets inflamed, then it may rupture and when that happens, a poisonous substance will spread into what is called the peritoneal cavity. The peritoneum is the membranous tissue which lines the abdomen. When the poison from the ruptured appendix spreads to the peritoneum, the results can be fatal and generally are. Do you understand what I am trying to tell you?"

"Well, Sir, it seems like you are saying I am going to die."

"Not yet, but in order to save your life, I will have to cut out your appendix before it ruptures."

"Will I be in much pain while you are operating?"

"We have ether, Doctor." the captain added hastily.

"You won't feel a thing. The ether will keep you asleep during the operation."

Jacques then said, "Then do it, doctor."

Andre edged towards the captain and said, "I have no proper equipment for an operation Captain."

The Captain replied, "I have a medical kit but it doesn't have any surgical knives in it."

"Well," said Andre. "I can use a knife from the gallery."

Then Andre turned to some of the seamen gathered around. "Will some of you assist Jacques to the salon?"

A few of the sailors helped Jacques to his feet and assisted him out of the door and took him to the salon.

Andre looked at the cook and said, "Now I will take a look at the knives in your galley, Cookie"

The two men headed towards the galley amidships and soon Andre was fingering the edges of the knives. He selected the smallest one he could find and turned to the cook and then drew a diagram of how he wanted the blade to look on a piece of paper and gave it to the cook. As the cook looked at the drawing, Andre said to him, "I want the blade of this knife made like this."

"Yes, Sir." replied the cook. "I will have the knife ready for you in an hour."

Andre left the galley and walked to the salon where Jacques was waiting with the other men.

"Well, Jacques, there should be no need for you to worry." Andre hoped that is own concern wasn't in his voice when he said that. Then he continued, "I feel that you should know what your situation is. If I don't operate and remove your appendix, you may die before we arrive in St. Pierre. The real danger at present is that your appendix may burst and if it does, there will be nothing I can do to stop the poison in your appendix from spreading to the membrane. If that happens, you will surely die before we get to St. Pierre and there will be nothing anyone there can do to save you."

"Are you saying that you should operate now, Doctor?"

"Yes, Jacques. I think that your appendix may burst in the next hour or so."

The seaman looked at Andre and gave a short smile and then said, "Then as I said earlier, operate, Doctor."

"I think there is something else that I should tell you first Jacques. I have never performed an appendectomy before. I only assisted on such an operation once."

"Do you know how it is done Doctor?"

"Yes, I remember the procedure well enough."

"Then I would be very grateful if you would take out my appendix, Sir. I would rather take my chances with your knife then with that damn thing inside of me."

"Very well, Jacques. I'll do my best."

The Captain entered the salon with a medical kit and gave it to Andre. He found the small bottle of ether and asked the captain to take the gauze out of the bag. He then showed the captain how he wanted the ether to be applied to the seaman's face.

Suddenly a voice was heard from on deck. The captain turned to his first mate and ordered, "Go up and see what the hell is going on up there."

"Aye, Sir," responded the first mate as he headed towards the hatchway.

He returned a few minutes later, his face showing fear. "Sir, you best come up. I can't describe what I have just seen."

The Captain, followed by the first mate went up the gangway and in less than a minute later, the first mate returned to the salon and said to Andre, "The Captain wants you topside right away, Sir.

Andre followed the first mate to the deck and saw the captain, his crew and passengers staring out to sea. Andre appreciated why the first mate had shown fear on his face when he had returned to the salon. As he joined the others staring at the horizon, he also realized why the first mate had also claimed he had never seen anything like it before. It was one of those freaks in nature that put seamen and passengers alike in a state of terror. Just astern of the boat about two kilometers away, off the boat's port bow, was a long thin twisting body of water reaching out of the sea and up into the dark clouds overhead.

"It's a damned waterspout." screamed out the Captain. "Those things will tear a boat apart in seconds."

"What's a waterspout?" cried out a passenger.

Andre replied, "It's a tornado at sea. I've never seen one before but from what I have read about them, they generally occur in the tropical seas during the warm seasons."

The first mate turned to the captain. "Sir. Have you ever seen one of these things before?"

The captain replied fearfully, "Yes, First Mate. Twice I have seen them but only at a distance and not this damn close."

Not another word was spoken as everyone on deck stared at the monstrous freak of nature while it whipped across the horizon, snaking about in one direction, then another. The agitation at the bottom of the column of water increased and as it did, it became apparent to the captain, and most certainly to everyone else, that the column of water was moving closer to their boat. Despite this fact, everyone's eyes were glued to the monster approaching them, as if mesmerized.

"Let's get this boat out of here." bellowed the captain as he pulled his eyes away from the waterspout. "First Mate. All hands on deck. Bo'sn, tell the Second Mate to take the watch forward. I want the jibs out, along with the three top mast stays."

The crew moved as one, everyone to his appointed post, as they had done before in emergencies. The sun began to hide behind the clouds as if attempting to avoid what was happening below. This resulted in the sky getting darker by the minute.

"Doctor Verlain." shouted the captain. "I'm afraid you will have to postpone your operation until we get clear of this waterspout."

"How long do you think that will be, Captain?"

"They never last more than half an hour."

"Well, Sir. The knife should be ready by then." responded Andre.

The captain noticed that the waterspout was turning towards the boat. He called out to the helmsman. "Twenty degrees to starboard."

"Aye, Captain." replied the helmsman.

The captain turned to the First Mate and yelled, "Prepare the mizzen staysails, the spanker and the gaff top sail for the turn to starboard, First Mate."

"You heard the Captain," yelled the First Mate to the men on the yard arms. "Get lively there."

Soon the clipper turned sharply to its starboard and headed against the wind. It was to no avail. The twister continued to dog them, moving closer by the second. Within five minutes, it had edged to within one kilometer of the *Marabeau.*

A roaring, hissing sound could be heard emanating from the base of the column as the agitated water was being sucked upwards into the giant vortex. The top of the twisting squirming column of water, which was at least twenty meters in diameter, had reached the low cloud above it. Andre and the others on deck were terrified as the swirling mass of water snaked and edged its way towards the boat.

Chapter Two

In less than a minute, a torrent of rain came crashing down on the sailing boat. “Captain.” yelled the first mate. “Best we take in the sails or they will be ripped to shreds.”

“Leave them be.” replied the captain.

“But Captain. The sails will be torn from the mast and if they’re not, then the masts will come down on our heads.”

The captain turned to his first mate and angrily shouted, “You bloody fool. If we turn in the sails now, we will lose our steering. I need full steering right now.” Then he turned to the helmsman. “Twenty degrees to the port!”

“Aye, Sir.” replied the helmsman as he turned the wheel a hard left.

The boat keeled to the left, its lower yardarms dipping into the crests of the high waves bushing up against the left side of the boat.

The first mate cried out beseechingly to his captain. “Sir. Can’t we take in the foresails and mainsails and rely on our jibs and mizzen for steering?”

“No.” replied the captain. “There isn’t time. That thing will be on us in minutes. We will have to keep ahead of that twister if we are to survive. I need all the sail I can get. I want all hands on the yard arms.”

The first mate yelled above the din. “All hands on the yard arms.”

The seamen scampered up the ropes and then with their feet on the ropes hanging below the yard arms, stood ready to furl the sails when and if the captain ordered them to do so.

"Get these passengers down below!" cried out the captain when he realized that they were still on deck. A number of seamen on deck began escorting the passengers down the gangway leading to the deck below.

Andre was still transfixed at what he was watching. Like the others, except for the captain, he had never seen such a display of the awesome power of nature, especially up close.

"Captain!" yelled one of the seamen. "The doctor is still on deck. The hatches are batten down. We haven't time to re-open one."

The captain looked in the direction that the seaman was pointing and then ran towards Andre. "Well Doctor, it looks like you are going to see this beast first hand. I can't re-open the hatches in time." The captain then turned to the boatswain. "Bo'sn! Get a rope and secure the doctor to the mizzen mast!"

The boatswain grabbed Andre by his arm and took him aft to the mizzen mast, picking up a line on the way. When they got to the mast, he stood Andre against the mast and told him to hold his arms in front of him with his hands covering his face. Then the boatswain began to wrap the rope around Andre's body and arms until all he could move was his head and hands. He then grabbed a piece of cloth from the sail locker and wrapped it around Andre's forehead in order to secure his head against the mast.

Andre watched the boatswain move away and return to amidships. Andre turned his head again and stared at the fearful thing that was approaching him. The waterspout was only a few hundred meters from the stern when he realized just how awesome this freak of nature really was.

High above the spindrift, which in itself rose higher than the top of the masts, the column of water swirled like a tornado. Searching as hard as he could, Andre couldn't see the upper part of the waterspout. The stinging spindrift lashed against his face. The boat began to lurch as if trying to escape the terrible fate that awaited it. The column of water loomed above him, a hundred meters aft of the stern of the boat. The mizzen yard swayed back and forth as if trying to break away from the mast. The roar of the twister seemed like a thousand people screaming as the wind blew the spindrift onto his face, tearing at his clothes.

The column of the water edged closer and Andre looked up the mast to which he was tied to and could see the twisting column of water leering over the top of the mast. The sails flapped about as if trying to tear themselves away from the yardarms. When he partially turned his head to look aft, he could barely make out the cauldron of boiling spume at the base of the twister because of the blinding spindrift. The boat began to twist and turn, its masts creaking and groaning under the strain.

Suddenly the stern began to rise upwards. It hung there as if suspended, and then it dropped down into the trough of a huge breaker. The wave loomed above the stern higher and higher, then crashed onto it with a mighty roar. Andre closed his eyes as the stern submerged under the monster wave. He felt the cold water rush over him in smothering caresses and while he held his breath, darkness surrounded him. It seemed like eternity before light appeared and when he finally opened his eyes and gasped for breath, the stern was rising upwards to meet the sky. He turned his head sideways and could just make out the column of water moving away from the boat's port side. Again the stern submerged under the sea but the water only rushed up to his chest. He watched with amazement as the water cascaded down the deck towards the amidships as the stern began its ascent. Then he heard voices behind him and he saw the boatswain approaching him with another man. When the two men reached Andre, the boatswain asked, "Well sir. What do you think of life at sea now?"

Andre sputtered out, "Give me land any day."

The two men laughed and then untied Andre and helped him walk towards the amidships. The boat was heaving but not as much as before. Andre could see the waterspout which was ahead of the boat by half a kilometer on the port quarter. Within minutes, the twister began to disintegrate. After a final twist, the column of water thinned out, then collapsed into the sea. The spray at its base vanished like a will-o-the-wisp. The sea suddenly calmed down and the wind blew gently against the sails.

Above the deck the seamen remained where they were while waiting for more instructions from their Captain.

Andre looked east and saw a white line of broken water on the horizon thrown into relief by the dense black clouds poised above it. It was moving closer to the boat.

"Captain." yelled Andre. "What's that off the port beam?"

The Captain looked through his telescope and then murmured softly as if to himself. "Looks like we may be in for a gale."

Andre thought of operating with the boat floundering at sea but his thoughts were interrupted with the Captain yelling orders.

"Quartermaster, call the second mate and tell him that I want the fore topgallant sails clewed up. First Mate, take eight hands and lower away the mainsail and get it secured fast. Bo'sn, haul all the jibs but leave the stayfore sail up. Now hop to it."

Then the Captain turned to Andre and said, "Doctor, you can operate now. I will try to keep the boat as steady as I can."

"Well, Captain, I will be able to manage but I will need some assistants for the operation."

"Can't spare you anyone, Doctor but you should be able to scrounge a few of the passengers to assist you." Then the Captain yelled to a seaman standing nearby. "You get the poop deck hatch uncovered so that the doctor can get below."

The seaman began taking the canvas off the hatchway while Andre watched the other seamen prepare for the oncoming storm.

Heavy planks were lashed over the main hatch, life lines were stretched along each side of the main deck and extra lashings were made on the anchors. Lashings were made on the life boats on the after skids and the forward deck house and lashings were bound around the spare spars on the deck.

The sea began to rise, the white caps of the waves were no longer a quiet profusion extending as far as the eye could see, but a tremendous expanse of tumbling water molded into cresting hills, with creamy foam breaking into spindrift as the roaring wind caressed and imposed its will on the surface of the sea that surrounded the boat. The boat was yawing badly in the ever increasing sea, under the press of the sail that she was carrying.

Suddenly the blast of the first squall hit the upper top gallant sails.

"Doctor!" yelled a seaman, "You can climb through the hatchway now."

Andre entered the hatchway and after one final look at the masts and white sails against the dark foreboding clouds, he descended, wondering all the time if he would ever ascend the steps again. He walked through the passageway until he found the salon. There on the table was Jacques who was being prepared for the operation.

The cook approached Andre and said, "I trust this is the way you wanted the knife formed, Sir."

Andre looked at it and nodded a sign of approval.

Andre turned to some of the passengers and yelled above the din of the storm, "I need three volunteers."

Three men stepped forward and edged closer to the table.

"Cookey!" yelled Andre. "I need four pieces of tin about an inch wide and six or more inches long."

"Aye, Sir," replied the cook. "I know where I can get them." Then he walked quickly through a hatchway leading towards the galley.

"All right." continued Andre "Secure Jacques tightly on the table so that he won't roll off."

Shortly, Jacques was well secured to the table and then Andre reached into the medical kit and took out the bottle of ether and some gauze.

"You!" he pointed to one of the men in the salon. "I want you to hold this gauze over his face like this."

Andre held the gauze over the face of the man on the table. Then he had one of the men reach into the medical kit and pull out an eye dropper. He took the eye dropper from the man's hand and pretended he was squeezing drops of ether onto the gauze. The man holding the gauze acknowledged the instructions with a nod of his head.

Soon the cook appeared with the pieces of tin and handed them to Andre who in turn bent the ends of them so that they looked like small garden hoes.

"These will be my retractors that will hold the skin, fat and muscles away from my work." he remarked to those watching him.

Outside, the storm continued to ravage the boat. The wind howled unceasingly in the rigging so that the woodwork of the boat vibrated like the wood of a stringed instrument. An occasional wave broke against the boat's side in a smother of water which precipitated over the decks while others heaved her up and over with a sickening lurch to starboard, only to roll back violently into the trough of the next oncoming wave.

Inside the boat, anything and everything that wasn't battened down securely, fell to the deck and then began rolling and sliding about the decks.

Andre turned to the three men and pointed to one of them and said "You will be called Number One. Your job will be to let the ether drip into the gauze every thirty seconds." The man he spoke to was a man of about thirty years of age.

Then he pointed to another and said. "You will be Number Two." He wasn't that much older. "You will hold the retractors in place as I will show you when the time comes."

Then he turned to another and said, "And you will be Number Three and will also hold two of the retractors in place when I give you the order." This man didn't like taking orders but in this case, he would make an exception. "Mainly your job will be to keep his blood from getting in my way."

"How will I do this?" asked Number Three.

"You will keep pads of gauze in there soaking up the blood." replied Andre as he pointed to the man's abdomen.

"Now," he continued. "I want all three of you to wash your hands thoroughly."

Minutes later, all four had washed and had put on makeshift masks over the lower half of their faces. Then they moved closer to the operating table. Andre poured some of the rum over the knife and retractors to sterilize them, then he poured the rest over the hands of number two and three and finally over his own.

"Number One," ordered Andre. "Put the gauze over his face and then begin putting the ether into the gauze." The man opened the bottle and dipped the eye dropper into it and drew the fluid into the dropper.

"Screw the top back on the bottle. That's right. Now hold the dropper upwards. That's it. Now when you are not dropping the ether into the gauze, hold the dropper upwards with your finger over the opening so that it doesn't evaporate." The man obeyed and then Andre continued, "Now put four drops into the gauze to start."

Number One followed Andre's instructions and a few minutes later, Andre took a stitching needle and stuck it into Jacques finger. There was no response.

"All right," said Andre as he glanced upwards past the ceiling. "I am ready."

Andre took the knife in his hand and deftly made an incision on Jacques' right side three inches long, just a few centimeters from his groin. The blade went through the skin and fat to the first layer of muscle.

Andre's blood spurted out and in seconds, his abdomen was covered in blood and was running onto the table and then to the floor. Andre took two of the retractors and pulled the skin and fat layers back.

"Number Two!" ordered Andre. "Hold these two retractors in place." The number two man did as he was instructed.

"That's it." responded Andre. "Further apart. Pull the layers further apart." he continued. "Number One!" he yelled, "Concentrate on the ether, not on what I'm doing. I don't want this man waking up with my hands in his guts."

"I'm sorry, Sir. It won't happen again."

"I can see the first layer of muscle," Andre mused to himself. *"Its fibers are running up and down."* Then he yelled, "Number Three! Get some of that blood out of there." Number three began stuffing the gauze into the opening and then drawing the blood-soaked gauze out again of the man's abdomen.

Andre shoved him away and then with the knife, began cutting into the muscle in the same direction of its fibers. The other men stared in fascination at the young doctor as he deftly cut through the muscles as if he was an old hand at it. "Number Two!" ordered Andre, "Get those retractors in past that muscle and draw the muscle away."

Number Two drew one of the retractors away then placed it down past the muscle and then drew one part of it away.

"Now that we have the outer muscle pulled away, I can get at the second one." Andre mused to himself, *"Since the fibres of the second one are running crossways instead of up and down, my next incision will have to be crossways."*

Andre took the knife and made another incision through the second muscle.

"Number Three!" yelled Andre, "Get that blood out of there!"

Number Three stepped in again and performed his duty even though it seemed like he was about to faint.

Andre reached for the other two retractors and edged them past the second muscles. When the second muscles were spread apart, Andre could see the glistening membrane which he had told Jacques earlier was the peritoneum.

"Number Three." continued Andre. "I want you to take these retractors I have in my hand and place them in the muscle."

Number Three stepped in again and grabbed the retractors.

"That's it. Now separate the muscle a bit further. That's better. Now keep the muscles apart."

Andre then reached around Number Three's arm and made another incision, this time through the peritoneum. "Number Two. Take the retractor in your right hand and place it past the second muscle and under the peritoneum."

Andre placed his finger under the peritoneum and lifted it upwards for Number Two to ease the retractor into place.

"Now pull away like you did with the muscle. That's it. Now the same with the other side." Again, Andre pulled the peritoneum upwards and the second retractor was used to pull it away.

"Number Three. You can take your retractors out of there now.... That's it. Now Number Three. Pull your retractors further apart.... That's it."

Andre realized that the gray-pinkish matter under the peritoneum was a portion of Jacques' large intestine.

He stuck his index finger into the bleeding wound and probed about trying to get the first part of the large intestine out.

"Damn it!" yelled Andre, "I can't get the caecum out."

Chapter Three

Andre probed on and suddenly, the intestine protruded outwards. He continued to push the intestine out with his finger and then he saw the appendix. With his left hand pushing the intestine, he reached for the appendix and guided it through the opening.

"Number Three! Get me the sutures from the medical kit. It looks like black thread."

Number Three came back with the sutures and handed them to Andre who then reached for them with his right hand.

"Now Number Three. I want you to hold this intestine up while I tie a knot in the suture."

"I can't." cried the man as he stepped back from the table.

"You will, damn you, or I will cut your heart out with this knife!" screamed Andre as he pointed the knife in Number Three's direction.

"All right," replied the man as he slowly approached the table again. "I'll do it."

"Now stick your hand in and keep the intestine up and out of the wound." said Andre as he guided the man's shaking hand towards the open, blood-filled wound.

When the man had the intestine in his hand, Andre placed a slip knot on the end of the suture and then slipped it around the base of the appendix next to the caecum. After tightening the noose so that it was tight enough to stop any blood that would pour out after the appendix was severed, he then took another suture and began tying the loop at the end of the second suture. He then placed the loop around the appendix and tied the knot just about a few centimeters above the first knot.

Number Three dabbed more gauze into the open wound.

"That's it." said Andre. "Now keep it packed in there and press it harder against the muscle."

Andre took the knife again and slipped it under the appendix between the two sutures.

"Number Three. Hold the appendix out with your two fingers. Whatever you do, don't squeeze it too hard otherwise you will rupture it and all the poison will run out of it and into this open wound."

Number Three held the appendix in his right hand and Andre with one quick movement upwards, severed the appendix.

Andre then turned the stump of the appendix inward after cutting the ends of the suture. This action he knew would prevent the caecum from adhering to the peritoneum. After checking the neighbouring parts of the intestine for perforations or accidental cuts, the bowel was put back into the abdomen.

While Andre was doing this, he said to Number Three who was just off to his right. "Thread the needle with a suture. I want the suture about twenty centimetres long."

Number Three went to work and shortly after that, he handed the needle and suture to Andre. After closing the peritoneum, Andre began to sew up the inner part of the wound.

"Number Two. Let the retractors slip over to the next layer as I keep sewing the bottom layer."

"While I am sewing the peritoneum, Number Three, you can thread me another needle that is the same length as the first one."

As soon as the peritoneum was sewn, Number Three was handing Andre another needle and suture.

"OK" continued Andre. "Thread this needle again. Same length as before."

Andre began sewing up the layer of muscle that was directly on the peritoneum. As soon as that layer of muscle was sewn, a needle and suture was handled to him and after instructing Number Three to thread the needle again, he commenced sewing the first muscle.

When he had completed that task, he took the needle and suture and sewed up the fat and skin just as Number Two slipped the retractors out on cue.

"Well gentlemen," said Andre with a smile on his face as he was finishing closing up. "You did a fine job assisting me."

"You did well yourself, Sir," exclaimed one of the assistants.

"Can I take the gauze off his face, Doctor?" asked Number One.

"Yes. Many thanks for keeping him unconscious."

Andre then turned to one of the men and said "Clean up will you after you have helped the others put Jacques in the Captain's bunk."

The men carried Jacques out of the room and after Andre put the knife, needles and ether into the medical kit, he went over to the liquor cabinet and helped himself to a bottle of gin. After taking a few mouthfuls, he felt he needed to get fresh air and despite the rolling deck and pitching deck, he managed to get to a hatchway. After repeated banging on the hatchway, the hatch was opened slowly. Suddenly a voice rang out. "Quickly! Get up here before the next wave comes."

The hatch was opened and Andre scrambled out just as it was slammed shut behind him.

"Quick, Sir!" said the voice "Get a hold of this line!"

Andre grabbed the life line and just as he got a firm grip on it, he saw the stern of the boat sink. A monster wave towered over the stern, then it came crashing down upon the deck, the wave passing over him, taking his sou'wester from his head with it. Finally when his face surfaced again, he saw the wave continue its journey along the upper deck, then, like a waterfall, cascaded down the steps leading towards the main deck. It smashed into everything that stood in its way and finally smashed headlong into the poop deck up forward; its power by then almost totally dissipated.

He looked up at the masts and he saw seamen on the yard arms attempting to haul in the sails. Nothing could he seen either ahead or astern of the boat except the spindrift.

"Doctor," a voice rang out. It was the captain pulling himself along a lifeline towards Andre.

Andre reached out and grabbed the captain's hand until the two of them were close together.

"Doctor, did I understand you to say that you once served on a boat?"

"Yes, that's right. I was an officer cadet in the French navy before I decided to go into medicine."

"Well I have another favor to ask of you when you finish the operation."

"The operation is finished and Jacques is in your bunk."

"That's fine, now back to my second request. It looks like we may flounder unless I get more sail hauled in. Could I impose upon you to go aloft and assist my men?"

"Yes, of course, Sir."

"Fine, Doctor. Report then to my First Mate at the main mast."

"Aye, Captain." replied Andre.

Andre pulled himself along the lifeline leading to the steps that went down to the main deck. After descending the steps, he crossed the deck just as a wave cascaded over the poop deck and down on to the main deck. The wave pulled him along the deck to the main mast.

"Mate!" he hollered out to the man by the mast who he recognized as the First Mate.

"Hello, Doctor!" the First mate replied. "The Captain told me he was going to ask you to assist us. The barometer has dropped to twenty-seven point fifty and is still dropping so if we don't get some of these sails in, we're finished."

"Yes, Sir. I understand."

"Good. You can come up with me to the main upper topsails."

Andre looked up and counted the sails and remembered that that particular sail was midway up the mast.

"Let's go then," yelled the mate.

The two men waited until the boat was high on a crest of a wave before scampering to the side of the boat. Just as another wave began to spill over the stern, the two men began climbing the ratlines. When they reached the main yard, Andre noticed the sails flapping violently.

"The helmsman is changing our heading, Doctor," yelled the mate. "As you know, sails are impossible to haul in if the boat is running with the wind."

Andre remembered back in his sailing days that when the sails, while ballooning up and cracking like a whiplash by the terrific force of the wind, the heavy canvas seemed to the touch as hard as iron.

Suddenly, because of the shift in the boat's heading, the wind blew the two men so hard into the rigging, they couldn't back their feet out of the ratlines to step upwards. Up above, the second yard in which the main lower top sail was suspended, was close to being torn away by the wind. Again they climbed and finally reached the main upper top sail.

The mate reached out with his foot to catch hold of the footrope, the line suspended below the length of the yard. When his foot caught hold of the footrope, he reached with his left hand for the hand line that was secured on top of the yard. Andre began to laugh when he saw the mate hanging in space but stopped laughing when he realized he would soon be hanging in space also.

The mate let go of the ratline and with a sudden leap, he headed towards the yard grabbed it and wrapped his right arm around it. His right foot reached the foot rope and then he wrapped his left arm around the yard, hanging on for all his worth.

The mate then turned to Andre and yelled, "OK Doctor, your turn now."

Andre wished at this point that he had been a coward and gone down to his bunk instead.

"Quickly, Doctor before the boat changes direction again."

Andre reached out with his left foot and after feeling the foot rope beneath it, he reached out with his left hand. When he felt the flapping line in his hand, he tightened his fist around it. It was in this position that he knew a sudden shift in the position of the boat in relation to the wind, would determine where he was going to be. He would be one of four places. Either still on the ratline, or the yard or if, as it has happened to less fortunate seaman, either on the deck, smashed to bits, or in the sea. Either one of the two latter alternatives was fatal.

"The boat is changing its heading!" yelled the mate as he held his right hand out to Andre.

Andre pulled his right foot from the ratline and edged it over to the foothold and just as it was on the line, the ratline began to pull him away.

"Let it go! Let it go!" yelled the mate.

For an instant, Andre released his hand from the hand line on the yard before he realized that the mate meant his hand holding the ratline.

Andre was almost horizontal to the deck when he felt another's hand grab his left hand.

"Let the right hand go," yelled the mate. "I can't," yelled Andre back.

"I have a good hold on you, Doctor. Let go of it."

Andre knew if he didn't make up his mind soon he would be stretched out to the point of no return. When he was sure the mate had a secure grip on his waist, he let go of the ratline with his right hand.

Suddenly the weight of his body fell outwards from the yard and his right arm swung out like a rope free in the wind. In seconds he was back to back against the yard and he felt another hand grab his right wrist. Another seaman had joined the two to assist the mate. Andre's right foot had pulled loose off of the foot rope and his left foot was slipping also. He turned his head and saw the mate standing to his immediate left. The mate looked past him to the man holding Andre's right wrist and yelled. "OK Pierre. Let it go, I still have this one."

As soon as Andre's right wrist was released, he began the return swing and shortly he was face to face with the yard. His right hand clutched at the yard and felt the hand line touch his fingers.

The mate smiled at Andre and laughed. "Is that how you used to get on the yards, Doctor?"

"No sir," he replied with a grin, his teeth clinched, "They used to hoist me up in a boatswain chair."

Both men laughed as they reached over the yard and they and the other men on the yard began to haul in the sail.

Andre leaned over the yard and grasped another hand full of canvas. With numb fingers, he clawed at the canvas, leaning as far forward as he dare, balancing his body against the ever heaving yard, his legs braced apart on the footrope.

The men had waited for a slight lull in the wind to ease the pressure of the wind on the sail so that a crease would be formed making it possible to force their fingers into the canvas. When the lull came, the men pulled up the canvas as one. After a struggle, the sail was gathered in and made fast in the gaskets.

"Now up to the top gallants', my lads," yelled the first mate.

The men reached for the ratlines one at a time and when Andre reached for it, he remembered what happens when seamen don't make decisions quickly.

He leaped into the rigging and was soon climbing up to the main lower top gallant yard. Despite his difficulty at climbing up the ratlines, he managed to get onto the yard without repeating his previous maneuver.

Again the men began to haul in the sail and half an hour later, it too was clewed up in the gaskets. Andre looked forward and saw that the sails on the upper fore mast were also being hauled in but he noticed that no one was working with the sails on the mizzen mast and that the foresail was not hauled in either. This meant more hazardous work ahead for him and the others.

Chapter Four

"Mate!" yelled Andre, "How come the mizzen sails aren't being clewed up?"

The mate yelled back. "Those aren't the only sails staying up. We are keeping the spanker and gaff sails up and the jibs and the fore stay sail aloft also.

"Is that usual for weathering out a storm?"

"Not usually, but the Captain has used this technique before. You know we have to have some sails up if we want to steer and if we don't steer, we will be at the mercy of the swells."

"Speaking of swells," Andre remarked, "How come we aren't sailing with the wind? At this rate, we are bound to capsize if we continue to move lengthways with the swells."

"That's right, Doctor," replied the mate. "But the captain has been trying for some time to get this boat to run crossways with the waves but until we get more sails hauled into the gaskets, the force of the wind will continue to blow us into the course of least resistance—right into the troughs, so it's up the ratlines we go again to the upper topgallant sail."

Again Andre and the other men climbed up the ratlines and moved deftly over the foot lines.

Never before had Andre been 24 metres up a mast that had swung in an arc of forty degrees both starboard and port. He looked down and watched a wave higher than any other approach the boat from the port beam. He wrapped his hands around the hand line and hugged the yard with all his might. The wave hit the boat broad side and blanketed the lower sails not already hauled in, with its spray. The boat reeled into the sea instead of yielding, then tipped to starboard and continued to roll. Andre could feel the force of gravity pulling him away from his grip on the hand lines. He was almost horizontal with the sea when he noticed the sea brushing against the mainsail and foresail yards. Just then, his feet fell from the footrope.

He was dangling feet first approximately 12 metres from the waiting waves. He knew he had to get his feet wrapped around the yard arm before the boat swung back over the crest of the wave and down the trough.

He began to lift his legs upwards and as he was doing so he could feel the boat starting its roll back to port. He knew that this roll to port would be his advantage because being on the starboard part of the yard arm meant that the yard would be coming to meet his legs. As predicted, his feet reached the yard and he wrapped them tightly around the arm just as the boat descended into the trough.

He watched with horror as the foresail which had not been hauled in, submerged under the sea.

"Damn!" screamed the first mate. "That damn sail will drag us over." He screamed out, "Second Mate! Cut the sail loose."

Andre looked down at the men on the foremast as they began to clamber towards the foresail yard.

The boat listed to port with the heavy sail acting as a pivot for the boat to swing about. Then he saw the men begin to hack at the gaskets holding the sail to the foresail yard. As they cut the ropes, the sail dipped further into the sea. Suddenly, after it had finally been cut free, the boat righted itself, and then headed into the wind.

The men on the main upper gallant yard arm pulled on the sail until it was in its gaskets. When some of the men began climbing down the ratlines, the mate turned to Andre.

"Doctor, you remain behind with some of the men to haul in some more sail."

"Aye Aye, Sir," replied Andre.

Andre watched the rest of the men climb down the ratlines. As they got closer to the deck, they began vanishing into the spindrift that covered the deck like a thick fog. Occasionally he could see the two helmsmen at the wheel, glancing at the breakers behind them. As the boat ran before the gale, the huge waves rose up, towering high above the stern, then the boat sank into a trough, the wave's crest threatening at any second to break over the boat in a devastating deluge of water. With the stern deep in the trough, a wave forty to fifty feet high crashed down on the deck as a boiling spume. The entire stern submerged with the bow high in the air. As the water on the upper deck cascaded onto the main deck, Andre saw with relief, the two helmsmen hanging on with dear life, their arms wrapped about the wheel to hold her steady. He thought to himself, *"What a risky trick that is, wrapping your arms around the spokes of wheel when a breaker smashes into it."* He knew that many a helmsman had his arms torn off when the wheel spun around after a hundred tons of sea smashed at the rudder.

The barque laboured heavily, with the deck awash as the sea broke over the rails. Another wave, bigger than the last, poised over the stern as if waiting for the right moment, then after carrying the boat forward, smashed onto the stern with the fury of a tidal wave. Again the stern submerged. The wave rolled over the entire boat, smashing the lifeboats against the shoulders of the davits. One of the boats was torn loose and dropped into the sea, tearing the davits away with it. The deck of the boat was one mass of liquid boiling fury.

Andre couldn't see anyone on the deck. He looked aft and saw the wheel spinning madly but no helmsmen. This was the finish of the boat. With no control at the rudder, she would become victim of any of the huge waves to come.

Then vaguely, he saw a man approach the upper deck from amidships. Where he came from Andre couldn't guess but the man headed towards the wheel. The man pulled himself towards the upper deck along the lifelines and finally reached the steps leading up from the main deck to the upper deck where the wheel was waiting. After braving the waterfall that crashed over the stairway, the man climbed them and reached for the lifeline attached to the railing.

Then the stern dipped just as the sea rolled over the upper deck. After the wave rolled over one deck and onto the other, the man again clambered up the steps and pulled himself along the lifeline towards the helm. He grabbed the helm and turned it to starboard and after a great effort, managed to keep the helm steady.

As the spindrift blew across the deck, Andre couldn't see anything below the first yard arm. He was grateful that the man at the wheel, whoever he was, who was attempting to get the boat to run on a different tact so that the waves wouldn't capsize her.

A short while later, he could vaguely make out the man at the wheel before the spray and spindrift cloaked him from view. The boat was turning so that it was now running lengthways with the swells. Andre climbed onto the yard so that he was belly down on it, and then wrapped his arms and legs about it for greater security.

The boat began to list. Andre felt the gravitational forces drawing him along the yard towards the end of it as the yard edged closer to the huge wave reaching up to pull him away. The white frothy crest of the oncoming wave towered and curled, poised high above the bulwark and then dropped below the hull of the barque as the boat rolled to leeward by the force of the wave. The body of water rolled under the keel and reappeared on the other side of the boat.

Suddenly, a bright flash of lightning with its simultaneous deafening clap of thunder, lit up the darkened midday sky. Within seconds, a torrential rain followed, lashing Andre unmercifully.

Andre pulled himself along the yard towards the ratlines. He knew that there was nothing that could be done by him alone. The other men on the yards had either climbed off of them or they had been torn from them, but they were no longer there.

In the equatorial zone, where the suction of the sun's heat draws water from the immense evaporating basin of the ocean, clouds form of such density that they are impenetrable by light, thus causing their undersides to be black. The minute drops of moisture in the clouds, swept upwards by the rising current of heated air from the surface of the sea, increase in size, sometimes several centimeters in diameter, until the shear weight of each drop causes them to succumb to gravity. The massive disintegration of the globules within the clouds liberates an electrical charge which then seeks out the highest free standing object below it.

Andre was lying next to that highest free standing object and knew that if he didn't get off the yard, the next bolt of lightning would search him out. He pulled himself along the yard until he reached the mast. Then he leaped to the ratlines and began climbing down them as fast as he could. While he was heading towards the heaving deck, he could see the torrents of water rushing along the deck, from one end to the other, sweeping the deck, searching for anything or anybody that wasn't properly secured.

The incessant wind from the east blew streaks of foam, torn from the mountainous crests, across the labouring vessel. As he climbed down the ratlines, he could see some of the men on the yard of the mainsail, their fingers tightly clutching the hand line lest they be seized by the waves immediately below them and pulled to their doom. Andre looked about and could see some of the men on the yards of the foremast. The halyards, severed by the force of the gale, steamed leeward and cracked like the ends of snapping whips.

While gingerly climbing down the ratlines, Andre knew that the worst of his climb down to the deck was yet to come. Each time the boat heeled over to meet the crest of a wave, the boat's railings dipped into the sea. He knew that if he was at the conjunction of the ratlines and the railing when that happened, the wave would sweep him away. If it didn't smash him into the superstructure of the boat while sweeping him along the deck and thusly killing him outright from the impact, he would be swept away from the boat and lost at sea.

He waited until the starboard stanchion dipped into the sea, and then he scrambled up the ratline to the stanchion on the port side. As he pulled himself up, he felt the boat drop to port and saw the sea coming up to meet him. He hung onto the ratline with his hands and his left leg draped over one of the ropes. He watched the sea as it rose to meet him knowing that he would not get to the deck on time. While holding on to the rope of the ratline as grimly as he could, the wave rushed over him and he felt his leg being pulled out of the ratline. All that held him to the boat was his fingers and they were slowly being pulled free from the rope. Just as he was about to be pulled from the ratline, he felt himself being hoisted out of the water as the port side ascended upwards again. He draped his legs over the stanchion and dropped to the deck and then scampered along the main deck and headed towards the poop deck. He didn't intend to climb the fore mast for if he was going to drown it would be in the comfort of his bunk. Just as he reached the steps leading to the poop deck, he saw a welter of foam, and a moment later a terrific wind slammed into the jibs up forward. He got up the steps just as the main deck plunged into the sea. He crawled over to the hatch leading down from the poop deck and slowly lifted the heavy iron hatch and slid into the hatchway just as a blast of water smashed into it. The sea caused him to tumble to the deck below. He stood up, partially daze and staggered along the passageway until he reached the salon.

In less than one hour, the time he had spent on the mast, the boat had scudded three times around the compass. He realized that the boat was sailing through a cyclonical gale, one that he had not experienced before.

He headed up forward towards his cabin and passed one of the seamen's mess areas. A glow from the blackened glass of the swaying oil lamp illuminated the damp and desolate surroundings. Steam rose from the wet and dirt-grimed clothes hanging between the tiers of bunks. He glanced inside but no one was about.

Andre continued through the passageway till he reached his cabin. He entered it and after climbing into his bunk, he felt for the straps that would tie him in. After locating them and securing himself he closed his eyes and eventually went to sleep. Outside, the wind and sea continued to rage in unabated fury.

It was hours before Andre heard a voice and felt a hand shaking his body.

"Wake up, sir." continued the voice.

Andre opened his eyes and looked into the face of a seaman and asked. "Where am I?"

"You are still on board the *Mirabeau*, Sir."

"We haven't sunk?"

"No, Sir," replied the seaman with a smile. "The captain is wondering if you would join him on the poop deck."

"All right. Tell him I will be right up."

Andre pulled himself from the bunk after untying the straps and had gone several metres down the passageway before he realized the boat wasn't rolling in the sea. He ran through the salon, through the passageway leading to the poop deck and bounded up the steps to the open hatchway. As he looked up, he could see blue sky and one of the mizzen sails reflecting the yellow glow of the sun.

While standing on the deck, he was amazed at the change from the last time he was there. The sea was calm, the breeze was gentle and warm and the late afternoon sun was shining as a golden ball in the sky.

"Good afternoon, Doctor," remarked the captain as he approached Andre.

"Good afternoon, Captain," replied Andre. "I hope you will forgive me for not going up the foremast."

"Of course, my boy," answered the Captain. "I appreciate everything you have done both for Jacques and the rest of my crew and passengers."

"How is Jacques, Captain?"

"Very well and he says he hopes you will visit him before you leave."

"Yes, of course."

"Incidentally, as Captain, I am authorized to return the fares of passengers. I hope you will accept this money as a token of my appreciation."

Andre accepted the money and then asked, "How close are we to Martinique?"

"There it is," replied the Captain as he pointed past the bow of the boat.

As the boat began its turn to starboard as per the Captain's orders, Andre could clearly see his destination off the port beam. The island, grayish in colour due to its distance from the boat was to his left with the volcano sticking its summit 1,397 metres into the blue sky.

An hour later as they closed in on the island, he mused to himself when looking at the volcano, *"It must be Mount Pelee."* He noticed with a little bit of concern that there were a few streaks of white vapor trails emitting from the crater.

On both sides of the volcano and running to the sea were massed golden-green regiments of sugar cane fields which appeared to go on endlessly for kilometres. Countless gorges and valleys ran down the mountain and dropped sharply into the sea. Further to the south of the volcano by about a kilometre or so was the city of St. Pierre, just as Andre imagined it. Two and three storey white buildings and houses with red tile roofs poked their way through the green trees.

He could faintly see the cobbled streets petering out up the slopes of the sharply rising volcano. The boat was turning into the harbour and Andre found himself staring at the city. From the sea, it appeared to back onto the southern foot of Mt. Pelee, rising in tiers from the harbour. He could hear the Captain bellowing out orders for the crew to prepare the sails for turning into the harbour. About half an hour later, the boat had dropped anchor and the passengers were preparing to disembark onto the cutters that had come out to greet the boat.

Andre rushed to the Captain's cabin, said his farewell to Jacques, and then he went to his cabin and packed his bag. Then he returned to the deck. "I wish to give you my thanks, Doctor and hope I have the good fortune to sail with you again." said the captain as he offered his hand."

"Thank you, Captain for the safe journey."

Andre climbed down the side of the boat and into the cutter waiting for him.

Half an hour later, he was standing on a wharf; the first time he had touched land in six weeks. He felt dizzy, a phenomenon characteristically common with persons who have been at sea for great lengths of time.

"Andre!" a voice called out.

He turned and there was Rachel running towards him. Her body was just as petite as when he last saw her in Paris and her brown hair was just as long as it was then. She outstretched her arms and when they touched, they embraced each other.

"Rachel, Oh Rachel!" Andre kept repeating.

Both hugged each other until a voice gently called out. "Your carriage is ready m'am."

"Oh, Andre, we feared for you when we saw the dark clouds out at sea. Was the sea rough?"

Andre laughed and said with a smile, "You could say that it was."

Together they climbed into the carriage and two men dressed in black drove the horses on. They drove along Rue Victor Hugo, the city's main street. Palm trees shaded the narrow, clean, brick-paved streets. Andre stared at the buildings on both sides of the street. The cathedral in the square was next to a park, He saw public gardens, the town hall and two leading banks, the Bank of Martinique and the English Colonial Bank. For the most part, the buildings on Victor Hugo were two and three storey affairs made of white stone with red tile roofs. The houses on the streets that intersected the main street; were all stone built and stone flagged, crowded in on each other, each with its wooden or zinc awnings painted red. The roads were of cobblestone and seemed to disappear into the green forests of the mountain. He thought to himself, *"I could really be happy living on this island."* He realized that wouldn't happen since he had a good job in Paris to return to.

Chapter Five

They crossed an iron bridge spanning the Roxlane River which intersected the city. Rachelle told Andre that most of the stone houses that clustered along the sides of the river where inhabited by the town's middle class Creole population. Their homes where built right down to the harbour which itself was a natural curving basin through which the entire life of the island funneled itself.

Andre remembered from Rachelle's letter that the bulk of St. Pierre's population of 26,000 men, women and children lived downtown in the mulatto quarter. The mulattos who with a century or more of breeding with sailors of the world had turned many of them almost white. Also intermarriage between Creole and Negro factions of the island had given many families different hues of white, brown and black.

Gradually the carriage headed up one of the cobblestone streets that intersected Victor Hugo. As they climbed higher up the hill, Andre noticed with interest that the small homes on both sides of the street seemed to be the same: tin-roofed houses surrounded by trees bearing ripening avocados, mangos, star apples, oranges, lines of grapefruit. Studded between the trees were tuffs of sugar cane, breadfruit plants, and tunnels of bamboo that protected most vegetables from the midday sun. Tethered around the bamboo were goats, cows, and small Creole horses.

Further up the mountain, the houses became sparse and the cobblestone road turned to dirt as the carriage continued its journey up a hill. They approached a darkened forest and soon were on a road that led through a tunnel of overhanging trees. The sky was almost blackened out as they drove through the dense forest.

Half an hour later after many twists and turns, they came into a clearing. As far as Andre could see, the clearing was like the lawn of a golf course. In the centre of it was a spacious house. It was not unlike one of the elegant chateaus that were so common in France. Behind the house, the sugar cane fields belonging to the Hayots extended part way up Mount Pelee and into a valley.

"Mother and Father are ever so looking forward to seeing you, Andre," remarked Rachelle as she snuggled up closer to him.

"I am looking forward to seeing them also, Rachelle."

"There is Father now," exclaimed Rachelle, as she waved her hand to him.

The greeting was acknowledged and soon the carriage was at the entrance where Marcel Hay was standing. He wasn't tall but he was stocky in build due to his work on his plantation.

"Father, do you still remember what Andre looks like?"

"Yes of course. How are you, my boy?" asked Marcel with a smile then said, "Do come in," as he shook Andre's hand. "Madame Hayot is looking forward to meeting you again."

The three of them entered a foyer where a man servant took Andre's hat and coat.

They entered a large room which Andre surmised was the drawing room. The furniture was French provincial.

"Andre," said Marcel. "You remember Madame Hayot."

"Yes Sir, of course. How do you do Madame Hayot?" replied Andre as he extended his hand to Marguerite Hayot as she sat on a sofa. She hadn't changed. She was still plump.

"I am well, thank you very much, Doctor Verlaine. I trust you had a satisfactory voyage."

"It was a bit exciting this morning."

"Yes, I understand the sky was rather overcast up north," she continued.

"Rachelle has told us that you must leave by the eighth," said Marcel.

"Yes sir, Rachelle and I must catch the *Rormania* back to France."

Marguerite turned a bit pale at Andre's remark which had referred to Rachelle as a fellow passenger. She knew that if her daughter left with Andre, she may never see her again.

Marcel turned to Rachelle and said "Would you show Andre to his room so that he may rest before dinner."

"Yes, Father."

Rachelle took Andre by the hand and led him upstairs to one of the guest rooms.

"Father and Mother have arranged a dinner in your honour tonight and a number of our friends will be attending," said Rachelle.

"That's very kind of them," remarked Andre as he embraced her again. "I've missed you, Rachelle."

"I missed you too, Andre."

"I noticed when I mentioned about taking you back to France with me, your mother turned a little pale."

"Oh you know how mother is," smiled Rachelle. "Always fretting about things she knows she has no control over."

"Well, we have only seven days in which to convince her that I really love you, Rachelle."

"You have already convinced Father. He says that the fact that you traveled all the way from France proves that you love me."

While the two talked, Rachelle's parents had a discussion of their own on the same topic.

"Marcel, I know that if we give Rachelle permission to marry that young man, we will regret it for the rest of our lives."

"Nonsense! It is obvious to me that that young man is genuinely in love with Rachelle and she with him. What more could you ask for our daughter?"

"Much more than he can give." replied Marguerite.

"More than love?" asked Marcel.

"Yes. What security can he give to her?"

"He's a doctor isn't he?" asked Marcel in a gruff tone of voice. "He's not a bum or one of our hired help."

"You know, Marcel, you have completely missed the point of what I am trying to say, haven't you?"

"If you would stop beating about the bush and get to the point, I might understand what you are driving at my dear."

"Very well," said Marguerite angrily. "Rachelle is our daughter, in fact our only child. When and if she goes and marries that young man and returns to France with him, who will inherit our plantation?"

"She will of course, unless you want me to disinherit her."

"Suppose they don't want to return and take over the plantation?"

"Well, it would solidify my belief in the young doctor as to his motives for marrying our daughter if they refuse to return."

"You mean you really think that he isn't just after the plantation?"

"Of course he isn't. He has a noble profession to pursue."

"I think he's after the plantation."

"Suppose he is." said Marcel. "Isn't that what you have always wanted—a young man to marry our daughter and help me manage the plantation?"

"Yes, but some local man whom we know."

"You mean some local man of whom you approve of and have personally selected."

"Now you know that isn't true, Marcel."

"All right then let me ask you this then. Is there any young suitor on this island that you have in mind to be our daughter's husband?"

Marguerite paused then replied "Yes there is."

"Who?" asked Marcel?

"Jean Aubrey."

"That dainty flower?" replied Marcel with a sneer.

"He is a very eligible young man and you know that is true."

"What makes him so eligible?"

"He comes from a very fine family."

"What makes you think that Andre Verlaine doesn't come from a fine family?"

"He doesn't."

"Who told you that?"

"Rachelle."

"She told you that? I don't believe it."

"Well she said he was an orphan and the he didn't know who his parents were."

"They could have been from nobility."

"Or felons in the streets of Paris."

"Marguerite! Sometimes you can be so trite. You make things into what they aren't. Besides, I would rather have Andre Verlaine marry our daughter before I would accept Jean Aubrey."

"Why?"

"Because Jean has told me on several occasions that his marrying Rachelle would amalgamate both our plantations into one large one. It's obvious to me that his interests lie with the amalgamations of our two plantations and not Rachelle."

Marguerite stood up and walked to the window to admire the sunset then said. "At least we know what his intentions are." She continued. "Further, he has been going with Rachelle for several years."

"And some mulatto wench in town." replied Marcel angrily.

"That's not true!" snapped Marguerite.

"How do you know? Did you ask him?"

"No, of course not."

"Well then, I suggest you let Rachelle make up her own mind without interfering."

"Very well, but I think you are wrong." replied Marguerite. Then she added, "We had better get dressed for our guests."

Several hours later, Andre was awakened by a knocking on his door. He opened his eyes and spoke up rather sleepily. "Yes, who is it?"

A voice belonging to one of the servants called out through the door. Dinner will be served in half an hour, Sir."

"Thank you. I will be down shortly."

Andre looked out the window and noticed the twinkling lights of the city in the distance, and he could just barely see the red streak on the horizon at sea where the sun had set.

Shortly after he was dressed, he left his room and walked down the hallway leading to the grand staircase. He could hear voices and knew the guests had arrived. As he descended the stairs, he heard Marcel call out to him from the foyer.

"Andre, my boy!" exclaimed Marcel as he approached the bottom of the stairs. "Come with me into the drawing room and meet our guests."

Andre and Marcel entered the room and there seated on chairs and sofas were twelve persons including Rachelle and her mother.

"Andre!" exclaimed Rachelle. "Come sit next to me."

"Let me introduce him to our guests first, my dear," said Marcel with a smile.

The men in the room stood up and Marcel said "Ladies and Gentlemen, Doctor Andre Verlaine."

The two then approached the nearest man. He was a man of about fifty years of age and possessed a large belly.

"Andre, I should like to introduce to you one of my dearest friends, Fernand Clerc. He is the owner of the largest sugar cane plantation on the island."

The two shook hands and Fernand said, "For a while I thought I wasn't going to have the largest one but now I am sure that that situation has changed, eh Marcel?" He knew about the plans of merging the Hayot plantation with the Aubrey plantation.

Marcel managed a smile then led Andre to the second guest. "This gentlemen is Andres Hurard, the editor of our newspaper in St. Pierre. His paper is called 'Les Colonies'."

"Doctor," said the editor. "I am indeed delighted to meet you. I have heard about your medical exploits."

"There're nothing to speak of, sir."

"Nothing he says." Turning to the others, Hurard continued, "Did you know that this young doctor took out a seaman's appendix during a severe storm at sea and all he had to perform the operation with was a knife from the galley and a few rather queasy passengers as his assistants."

"And some ether," laughed Andre.

"Then let me be the next to shake his hand," said a rather pudgy man walking to Andre. "I am Roger Fouche, the Mayor of St. Pierre."

Andre extended his hand and answered. "Delighted!"

Marcel then led Andre to another man who approached them with a woman in arm.

"This is Doctor Guerin and his wife. They own the sugar refinery on the island."

"You must tell me how you did that operation doctor." laughed Guerin. "Somehow, I must have missed that technique in medical school."

"You didn't miss much then doctor." replied Andre with a laugh as he kissed Mrs. Guerin's outstretched hand.

"Andre," continued Marcel, "These three ladies sitting on the sofa, are Mrs. Clerc, Mrs. Fouche and Mrs. Hurard."

After being introduced to the women, Andre was led to two men in clerical robes.

"Andre, this is Father Mary who is one of our most outspoken critics of Voodooism."

"Father Mary." said Andre. "You must tell me about Voodooism one of these days."

"Of course, my son."

Rachelle's father turned to another cleric and said, "And this gentleman is one of the island's leading authorities on volcanoes."

"That's very good to know." said Andre with a smile, "because I have a question to ask about Mount Pelee."

"Yes, my son?"

Andre continued. "I noticed vapor trails coming from the volcano today. I always thought that Mount Pelee was extinct."

"It's very much alive, Doctor." replied Father Roche.

"Nonsense!" retorted the editor.

The priest gave the editor an inquisitive look and then said, "Perhaps you can explain what has been causing the rumbling noise for the past week."

"Professor Gaston Landes," began the editor, "says that we are on one of many islands that comprise of a chain of extinct volcanoes and that every once in a while, the earth trembles because we are also in an earthquake belt.

"Our island is one of a chain of smoldering furnaces about to burst into flame." remarked the priest.

"And it appears that one of those smoldering furnaces has already burst into flames." added Marcel.

"You mean, Pelee?" asked Andre.

"No. I mean Mount Soufriere on the island of St. Vincent. Surely you must have seen its smoke when you were passed the island."

"No." replied Andre. "It was so stormy and I was so occupied that I wasn't aware of any volcano erupting."

Father Roche continued. "Pelee's been smoking for some time now but I'm sure that it will erupt soon. It has erupted on two occasions in the past; that is since the eighteenth century. Once in 1790, it sputtered a thin scattering of ash over the immediate slopes of the crater, then in 1851, it erupted after a week of rumbling, followed by a column of ash which drifted down on top of the city, giving it a mantle of white."

Fernand Clerc smiled at Marcel and added, "About a month ago, I took my wife and two children to the summit of Pelee for a picnic. As you all know, there is a small lake in the centre of the crater. As we sat at the edge of the lake, we noticed a small wisp of smoke coming from the other end of the lake. We walked around the lake to see what it was and a breeze came up and blew acrid smoke into our faces. Our eyes began to water and we began choking on what was obvious sulphur-bearing gas. We began to run away and as we ran, a black fountain of ash shot into the air and fell lazily across the lake. Needless to say, we chose not to hang about checking it out."

"What do you think it was?" asked the editor.

"Probably some hot mud!" exclaimed Father Roche.

"Well," continued Fernand. "I went up the mountain again a few weeks ago and looked into the crater to see if any changes had occurred."

"Were there?" asked Father Roche.

"To be sure, there was. The placid surface of the lake had become a black mixture of bubbling and boiling mud; rising and puffing. From time to time, jets of white vapor and scalding water escaped and then fell back brusquely into the caldron. The island in the middle of the lake was completely submerged beneath all this mixture."

"How come you didn't report what you had found?" asked Mayor Fouche.

"I did. I sent a letter to Governor Moutter and all he did was to ask me to let him know if the situation gets worse."

"Unfortunately, his office is in Fort du France and therefore he isn't really that concerned." said Father Mary.

"Dinner is served, Madam," the butler's voice called out.

Everyone went into the dining room and for the next few hours, they all enjoyed the dinner and conversation. After dinner Margerite stood up and all the men rose and then she said. "Perhaps the ladies can join me in the drawing room for tea while the men drink their wine."

The women went into the drawing room leaving the men to their wine and cigars. The men began conversing as soon as the women left.

"Gentlemen, I wish to propose a toast to my daughter and her young man, Andre on their forthcoming marriage."

"Hear Hear!" exclaimed some of the others. The men stood up and raised their glasses towards Andre.

"Thank you Gentlemen," replied Andre with a smile as he raised his glass towards Marcel.

In the drawing room, Marguerite was pouring tea when Mrs. Clerk asked Rachelle when she had met Andre.

"About a year ago." replied Rachelle. "He's come here to marry me."

"That hasn't been decided yet, dear," said Marguerite.

"It is as far as I'm concerned," replied Rachelle acidly.

Marguerite turned to her cronies and remarked sadly. "It's a shame that one's children are always making plans to marry without first consulting with their parents."

Rachelle got up and while walking out of the room, turned and then said for all to hear. "It's a shame that one's parents are always making other plans to marry off their offspring without first consulting with them."

Rachelle and her mother eyed each other, waiting for the other to speak. Neither did. Rachelle turned and walked briskly out of the room.

Chapter Six

In the early morning hours of May 2nd, Mt. Pelee emitted a column of grayish-white smoke which rose thousands of metres into the air. No one saw the smoke rise from the crater as it was unaccompanied by neither fire nor thunder, but a few watched it descend upon St. Pierre and the surrounding countryside. Swiftly and silently the ash fallout fell to earth and in a few short hours everything for miles was covered with a blanket of ash. The trees, fields, houses, streets and even the sea for many miles out, were all covered with the grayish-white ash that was in some places, several centimetres thick.

Andre heard the distant toll of the bell of the Cathedral of St. Pierre resounding across the wakening city and up the hill where the Hayot chateau stood. He looked at his watch and noted that it was six o'clock. He was just pulling himself out of bed when he heard a commotion downstairs. It wasn't clear enough to him so he opened his door a bit. The voices were excited and seemed to move towards the western portion of the house.

He walked across his room and looked outside his window. He too became excited when he saw the white countryside. As far as his eyes could see, even as far as the horizon where the sky met the sea, everything was white as if snow had fallen earthward. He picked up a handful of ash from the balcony then hastily went inside as a gust of wind blew some of the ash into his room.

Andre dressed and went downstairs and joined Rachelle and her mother for breakfast.

"What do you think of our snow Andre?" asked Rachelle laughingly.

"For a few moments, I really thought it was snow," replied Andre with a smile. "I suppose there are quite a few people surprised this morning."

"Yes, I think all my children will be very excited today," said Rachelle.

"Your children?" asked Andre as he choked on his coffee.

"Yes," laughed Rachelle, "The children in the orphanage."

"Oh." said Andre somewhat relieved.

"Speaking of orphanage, I must hurry or I will be late."

"Late?" asked Andre.

"Oh yes, I forgot to tell you. I work at the orphanage in St. Pierre."

"When will I be able to see you again?"

"Why don't you pick me up for supper, Andre and we can spend the evening together in the city?"

"OK. That will be fine dear," replied Andre."

Just then, there was sound of bell tinkling at the front entrance.

"We have someone coming for breakfast," said Marguerite.

A young man entered. He was in his twenties and clean shaven.

"Jean! What a surprise," exclaimed Rachelle. "Andre, let me introduce you to Jean Aubrey. He's a very good friend of ours."

Andre stood up and shook Jean's hand then asked, "Have you lived on the island very long?"

"All my life," answered Jean with a smile. "In fact, my plantation is bordering next to the Hayots."

"Jean." said Rachelle. "Could you please be a dear for me and show Andre around the city. I have to work at the orphanage and won't be able to be with him until this evening."

"Yes of course!" replied Jean. Then while facing Andre, he said, "I think you will find our island a fascinating one."

"If this ash is a sample, I will be very fascinated."

Marguerite turned to Jean and said, "I certainly hope that this ash is all we are going to get from Mount Pelee." There was a distant look of fear on her face that didn't go unnoticed.

"Mother," said Rachelle. "You always worry about little things." Then she turned to Andre and kissed him saying, "Remember dear. At six o'clock at the orphanage. Jean, you will take him to the orphanage, won't you?"

"Yes, of course." replied Jean with a warm smile.

Without another word, she left the room and Andre could hear her call one of the servants to fetch the carriage.

An hour later, Andre and Jean were driving through St. Pierre in Jean's carriage drawn by a gray horse.

"You will find St. Pierre a fascinating city at night Andre." said Jean. "You should get Rachelle to show you our high spots."

"I will ask her tonight," answered Andre, then he continued, "Have you known Rachelle long?"

"Ever since we were children," replied Jean.

Soon they were heading out of the city and when they reached the outskirts Jean turned to Andre and said, "I thought I would show you one of our fishing villages."

"What's it called?"

"Le Prechure." said Jean. "It's eleven kilometres to the north of us."

An hour later they reached the village and Jean pulled up the carriage beside a priest walking towards a church. He was in his fifties and fairly stout. His beard and mustache were grey.

"Father, Roberto," yelled Jean.

The priest turned around and answered, "Jean, my son. I haven't seen you in over a year."

"I have been very busy Father," replied Jean. "Father, may I introduce you to Andre Verlaine. He has just arrived from Paris."

The two shook hands then Jean said, "Andre and Rachelle Hayot are going to be married in a few days."

"But Jean—I thought you and—well I guess the lady can change her mind. I am sorry Jean." The priest gave a small wink to both men.

Andre turned to Jean and said, "I didn't know that you and Rachelle were engaged."

"Actually we were never formally engaged."

"I am sorry Jean," said Andre. "I seemed to have stepped in on your love life."

"It's OK Andre. Don't fret about it."

The priest turned to the men and said, "Why don't you two wait for fifteen minutes and I will join you and perhaps I can offer you some coffee at my house."

"Thank you, Father," replied Jean.

The priest continued, "Well Gentlemen. It's midday now so I will have to gather my flock in and reassure them that there is nothing to worry about with all this ash covering everything. I will see you then in fifteen minutes."

"You can reassure me also that everything will be OK while you're at it," exclaimed Andre with a smile.

Both laughed and the priest walked to his church, in moments the bell was ringing and the townspeople were gathered around the square facing the church.

"My friends," started the priest in soothing tones. "You have nothing to fear. Mount Pelee has spewed forth white ash. It's nothing more. Soon, the winds will blow it away and everything will be green again."

"But Father," cried a man in the middle of the crowd. "This has never happened before."

"But it did, many years ago, my son."

"Never like this Father," cried another.

Two hundred of them, men, women and children stood in the square waiting for further words of comfort from their priest. The priest placed the small statue of the Virgin Mary he had in his hands on the ground near his feet and knelt down to pray. The others followed his example. They had just knelt when a voice in the rear of the crowd screamed, "Look at the street behind us!" At once, everyone stood up and turned to face the street behind them.

A trickle of lava and steaming mud was nosing slowly into the village. The lava and hot mud, now black as it was cooling, moved slowly since its force was spent, having traveled eight kilometres from its source at the summit of Pelee. The sight of it seeping into the village, knee high and gently steaming, brought panic to the villagers. They ran in all directions except towards the approaching lava.

"We must flee to St. Pierre!" screamed out the priest.

The villagers as one; began to move in the direction of the coastal road leading towards St. Pierre. Jean offered to take a number of the babies in his carriage for some of the women. For several hours, they all traversed along the long twisting road leading to the city. Behind them the small statue of the Virgin Mary in the square toppled into the lapping mixture of lava and steaming mud to become part of the mixture spreading down the streets of the abandoned village.

On the peak of Mt. Verte, three kilometers south of St. Pierre, Father Roche, viewed Mt. Pelee with professional interest. The tall Jesuit had spent his lifetime studying the cause of volcanic disturbances in the Caribbean. For three weeks he had been observing Mt. Pelee and its behavior. Every few days, he climbed the pumiced slopes of the Mount Verte to look at Mt. Pelee. He knew the geology of the volcano well.

Pelee, like the other four hundred smaller mountain peaks of Martinique, was composed almost entirely of volcanic material that had been thrust up through fractures in the sea bed when the earth's crust was cooling. Pelee, one of five hundred volcanoes around the world that have been active in historic memory, lies in the centre of one of the great volcanic belts that circle the oceans of the world. The largest of these is the ring that surrounds the Pacific. Starting at the South Shetland Islands, several miles south of Cape Horn, the chain extends up the west coast of South America, Across Central America and on up through the North America continent. In Alaska, it crosses the Pacific to the Aleutian Islands. From there it sweeps on to the eastern seaboard of the Pacific, taking in Japan, Formosa, the Philippines, the Solomon Islands and New Zealand, before finally ending at Mount Terror on the Antarctic continent. In all, it stretches for nearly twenty-five thousand miles, embracing over two hundred million people. Eastward from the Indian Ocean, another belt extends through Sumatra and Java. It is the most active of all the chains. At that location, over one hundred volcanoes are constantly displaying nature's energy. It is here that the natives live beside the gigantic boilers that bubble and regularly spew out liquid rock and gases from the very core of the earth.

The Atlantic is edged on three sides with a volcanic chain. It starts on the far north, traveling through the peaks of the Azores, the Canary Islands, the Cape Verde Islands, Ascension, St. Helena, and Tristan da Cunha. On the western side of the ocean are the volcanoes of the West Indies. They include the peaks of the Saba in the north, rising nearly three thousand feet above sea level, to Grenada in the south, from whose peak on a clear day the outline of the South American coast is visible. In the centre of this Caribbean branch of the great Atlantic belt is Mt. Pelee.

From his position, on the summit of Mt. Verte, Father Roche looked out across the jungle vegetation to the volcano. Below him was a patchwork of swamps, streams and small rivers. Sprinkled among them were plantations and hamlets. The rotting steaming jungle rose to a deep collar of shrub-covered lava rock. Above the collar stretched the neck of Pelee, short and massive, ending at the open mouth of the crater.

He watched the crater discharge more of the white ash which was carried by the wind past the neck of Mt. Pelee and down upon the jungle like a fresh snowfall. As the priest was looking over the jungle he was unaware of the small party of men and women climbing up a trail, hidden by the trees.

The group was led by an anxious bride groom who was searching for his bride-to-be and the old Voodoo priestess who was to give Voodoo instructions to the girl in the art of love and customs of marriage. The girl had spent the previous week in the cave of the old woman. Several hundred metres from the cave, the party found the bodies of both women, their bodies hideously scalded. They lay beside a steam vent which had burst open by the trail just as the two of them passed by it. Mt. Pelee had claimed its first victims.

Father Roche meanwhile tried to find a way in which he could calm the fears of his parishioners in the mulatto quarter. They were a superstitious lot and it would require a great effort for him to convince them that the Devil was not about. His parishioners had always thought the Devil lived just below Pelee and that the fire and smoke coming from the crater was really the Devil's breath.

Outwardly, the volcano offered the traditional conical shape of volcanoes the world over. In the last twenty-four days it had acted like any other volcano stirring from sleep; emitting dust and ash in a sudden up-rush of gas and steam, and at night lighting up the sky with brilliant lightning flashes.

There are many kinds of volcanoes. Those of Hawaii-Mauna Loa and Kilauea had given their names to the most spectacular kind of volcanic eruptions. When they erupt, they send great fountains of flaming debris cascading into the sky. Mauna Loa, the largest volcano in the world, rises from her seventy-mile-wide foundation to protrude nearby fourteen thousand feet above the level of the sea. While on the rampage, her throat glows, fanned by the mighty bellows working away on the ocean bed. Around its peaks miniature tornadoes stalk, fanned to life by the intense heat pouring out of the crater and meets the cold air at the heights of the summits.

When Father Roche was a young man, he remembered seeing another type of volcano in Sicily. It was Stromboli, a natural lighthouse familiar to the Mediterranean traveler for centuries; in fact it had been glowing since the dawn of history. Its discharge was slight, not unlike the way Pelee had been discharging. The volcanic type is explosive and sudden, caused when a plug of lava that has blocked a volcano's throat is burst by the pressures beneath and a mass of solid liquid rock is hurtled into the area in great clouds of vapor and dust. The Icelandic kind of eruption occurs when billions of tons of fluid lave pour steadily over thousands of square miles of countryside and sea, wasting everything it touches. Father Roche knew of the kind of eruption that took its name from Solfatura in Italy. The last time its crater ejected lava was in the Twelfth Century. Since then it had only discharged gases and an occasional trace of ash.

Andre and Jean decided to bypass the normal route through to the city by transversing the sugar cane fields. The priest had the babies transferred to another carriage heading into the city.

Jean took his carriage on a seldom used road which headed in the direction of the city. They had been on the short cut about half an hour when Andre heard distant voices yelling. When Jean heard the voices, he stopped the horse.

"What do you think it is?" asked Andre.

"I'm not sure but it appears to be coming from the forest over there," said Jean as he pointed to an area east of the road.

Jean tied the horse to a small tree and then the two men walked through the forest and as they approached a clearing, they could hear a distinctive rumbling sound nearby. Soon they came into a clearing. What they saw shocked both men. A sea of boiling mud was racing down the slopes of the mountain and spreading across a valley ahead of them.

Firmly trapped in the mud, about a hundred metres away, were seven men on horses. Struggling to get clear, they stood no chance against the tidal wave of mud that was going to overwhelm them. All they could do was cry pitifully for help.

No matter how Andre and Jean tried, there was no way that they could reach the trapped men. Both men watch with anguish as the last of the screaming horsemen and their horses were swallowed by the steaming mass.

Both of the men ran back to the carriage, aware that the mud would engulf them if they remained and continue its journey to the sea. They climbed into their carriage and raced to the city to warn Mayor Fouches of the danger. There was no sound from the wheels of Jean's carriage as the sound was muffled in the ash on the streets. Finally they reached the city hall and while a woman looked after the babies in the carriage, Andre and Jean were ushered into the Mayor's office.

"Gentlemen!" said the Mayor as he stood up to greet them. "What brings you two to my humble office?"

"We thought it best to advise you that there is lava pouring into the town of Le Prechure and seven men on the Laveniere estate have been buried in a flow of mud coming down one of the valleys," replied Jean.

"What has happened to the villagers?" asked the mayor.

"They are on their way to the city," answered Andre.

The mayor walked over to the door to his office and called to an assistant. The assistant, a mousy type of man stood at the door.

"Send for the military commander and then tell him I want the villagers from Le Prechure coming into St. Pierre to be quarantined in the town hall compound."

The captain of the *Mirabeau* was heading out to sea for his journey back to Paris when he noticed with curiosity that thousands of dead fish were floating on the surface belly up. The white ash on the surface he could understand but not this new phenomenon of the dead fish. What he didn't know was that Pelee extending 10,000 feet to the sea bed, had twitched at its base and sent a shock wave hurtling to the surface that had killed everything in the sea for several square kilometres. In the process it had also damaged the underwater telegraph cable from Martinique to Dominica.

As the captain focused his telescope on the shoreline, he watched in awe as the steaming lava and mud poured through the streets of Le Prechure, setting some of the houses aflame. When the lava reached the sea, large columns of steam rose hundreds of metres into the air.

Chapter Seven

Andre and Jean left the Mayor's office after completing their mission of informing the mayor as to what they had seen and headed towards the mulatto quarter. It was late afternoon and there was an hour to kill so Jean though he would show Andre some of the sights. An hour later, they drove to the orphanage where Andre was to meet Rachelle. "Andre," said Rachelle. "I am very sorry but I have to spend the evening here until midnight. Some of the children are ill." André was disappointed but he understood and after a kiss, he said that he would pick her up at midnight. Jean headed the carriage down the street towards the center of town. "Andre!" said Jean. "I have just the solution for our evening. We can visit some of the night clubs in the mulatto quarter. They have some fantastic dancers here that would make even an old man come alive again if you get my meaning."

Suddenly, a low rumbling noise could be heard coming from the direction of Pelee. The two men looked up and saw a column of white smoke pouring out of the crater. They watched with astonishment as the cloud of smoke and vapor rose thousands of metres into the air, then it spread across the sky like an umbrella. Minutes later, the crater emitted no more ash but both men and the rest of the populace stared as the white cloud slowly descended down over the city. Within minutes the sulfur-smell choking ash fell on the city. Everyone scampered indoors. Andre and Jean ran into one of the stores just as the doors were being closed. Andre coughed and gasped then asked, "Jean, has this ever happened like this before?"

"No." replied Jean. "At least not in my lifetime."

For fifteen minutes the snow-like substance fell on the streets and buildings. When it finally let up, both men left the protection of the store and climbed back into Jean's carriage.

"Listen, Andre. I know just the place where we can have a good meal."

"Great." exclaimed Andre who would go anywhere to eat as he hadn't eaten since early morning. The carriage plowed through the freshly fallen ash, the white substance swirling about the wheels of the carriage and the horse's hooves. It wasn't until eight in the evening before they left the cafe where Jean had earlier suggested they eat. Then they went to the 'Latin Club' which was located in the centre of the mulato quarter and where they could sample some of the island's finest wines. In the centre of the club, past all the smoky haze, was a large circular stage, half a metre in height, which in turn, was surrounded by small tables, each with little soft-glowing lamps on them.

After getting a table close to the stage, Andre remarked, "We'll get a good view of White Flower when she comes on stage."

"White Flower?"

"Oh yes," grinned Jean. "She is what every man in this room dreams of when he goes to bed."

"I dream of Rachelle."

"Rachelle is a beautiful girl, Andre but believe me when I tell you that after you have seen White Flower—." Jean paused for effect and then said, "Let me put it this way. You will marry Rachelle but you will still dream of White Flower." After ordering a bottle of red wine, Jean continued. "Her real name is Monique Rousseau. Her mother was a mulato seamstress and her father was a white trader but she's more white than black and she's certainly more woman than most."

Suddenly there was a fanfare of musical instruments from the six-piece band coming from the other side of the room. Everyone looked up as if one and then focused their eyes on the woman approaching the stage from the direction of the band." White Flower! White Flower!" cried out the patrons in unison. Andre began focusing his eyes on the subject of their attention. She was around twenty, he figured. Her skin was almost white, just as Jean had stated. Her legs were long and smooth and the rest of her body was proportionally right. Her breasts were rounded like tantalizing grapefruits. Her hair was black and long but next to her right temple, was a white flower. Now he knew why she was called White Flower. The tempo of the music slowed down and then she began to dance in the centre of the stage; gyrating her hips slowly, each move calculated to arouse every man in the room. Within minutes, the tempo quickened and then the silks covering her body flew in all directions, her arms and legs almost following suit. Her black hair swirled about her face, covering her dark piercing eyes for an instant before the reflection of the lamps brought them to life again. She gazed about the room at each miniscule stop in her rhythm causing each man in the room to believe that she was giving him a personal glance. Everyone was chanting her name, as if it was part of a pagan rite. Within ten minutes, her dance was over. She flew off stage and in seconds, vanished behind a curtain behind the band.

After the handclapping and cheering subsided, Jean leaned towards Andre and said, "Would you like to meet her?"

"Would I?" remarked Andre. "Is the sky blue? Are trees green? Would I like to meet her? The answer to all three questions is obvious, is it not?" laughed Andre. Jean smiled and after writing a note, he handed it to one of the waiters.

A few minutes later, White Flower parted the curtain and approached their table. Both men stood up as she neared the table and Jean smiled and said, "Your dance was beautiful Monique, as always."

"Thank you, Jean," replied Monique as she extended her hand which Jean kissed gently.

Andre, not to be left out asked, "Would you do us the honour of joining us at our table?"

"Thank you very much," said Monique as she smiled at Andre.

"Oh. Excuse me, Monique," said Jean apologetically." May I introduce Doctor Andre Verlaine? He has just arrived from Paris and is staying with the Hayots."

"Delighted, Doctor!" said Monique as she seated herself at the table with the assistance of Jean.

Andre said, "I admired your dance, White flower."

"Just call me Monique. My friends always do."

"Thank you, Monique," said Andre who was very pleased at being referred to as a friend.

"I have heard all about you, Doctor and your fascinating operation at sea." "That certainly got around didn't it."

"Everyone is talking about it, Doctor."

"Just call me Andre. All my friends do."

Monique smiled and said "Thank you, Andre." Then she turned to Jean and asked, "What have you been doing lately, Jean? I haven't seen you for a while. Have you been courting Miss Hayot as before?"

Jean blushed at that last question and said. "As you know, Rachelle and I had planned to be married some day, but she fell in love with a doctor in Paris, in fact the very doctor sitting with us."

Andre turned to Jean and said, "I really am sorry about that, Jean." "That's OK, Andre," replied Jean. "I won't say the best man won but rather that the lady has decided to change her mind."

"That seems like the right thing to say," answered Andre with a smile.

"Back to your question, Monique," said Jean. "I have been working pretty hard on the plantation. Since Father died, I have had to manage the plantation myself."

"Yes I heard about your father," said Monique rather sadly.

"What have you been doing, Monique, aside from your magnificent dancing?"

"I am getting pretty involved with politics as you may know."

"So I have heard."

"Politics?" asked Andre in a rather surprised voice.

"You find it unusual for a mulatto to be in politics?" asked Monique.

"No! No!" answered Andre quickly. "In fact if you are running for office, you have my vote."

"Thank you, Andre, but I'm not running for office. I am Senator Knight's secretary."

"Senator Knight?"

"Oh yes, I forgot; you aren't aware of our island's politics," replied Monique.

"Senator Knight," said Jean, "is active in the forth-coming elections. "

"Well I can understand why a white man would have a charming girl like you as his secretary," said Andre with a smile.

"Senator Knight is a black man," said Monique. "In fact he is probably one of the blackest men on the island.'

"Pigmentation-wise that is," added Jean.

"Yes," laughed Monique, "although I think that some of his opponents might think his heart is the same colour as his skin.

"Senator Knight must be a very talented man to have won a seat in the senate as a black man," said Andre.

"Well you mustn't forget that the area that he represents is almost entirely mulatto and if the mulatto people have a choice of electing a white or black man, they will choose the latter," said Jean.

"Senator Knight," said Monique, "didn't win just for that reason." Then she continued, "He used to be a worker on a plantation and now he owns one of the largest on the island."

"I hear he is one of the hardest task masters of all the plantation owners," added Jean.

"That's true," said Monique. "He feels that because he is black he has to compete against the whites. He isn't accepted into their clubs or homes so he competes against them in the two ways that he can be their equal. Politics and business."

"Those are two ambitions that are great equalizers in society," laughed Andre.

"Amedee, that is Senator Knight, is trying very hard to control this forth-coming election despite the fact that there is a split in the Radical Party," said Monique. "He has been hoping that the smoke from the volcano will bring in the party supporters from the countryside."

"Does he not have enough supporters here in town?" asked Jean.

"It's not that," answered Monique. "It's just that the party seems to be putting two candidates into the race,"

"Who are they?" asked Jean.

"Percin and Lagrosillere."

"Who is Lagrosillere?"

"A nobody," replied Monique,

"What will happen to Lagrosillere if he loses?"

"Oh, he has stated that he will withdraw from the second ballot if the results of the nomination are inconclusive. And if he does this, he has been assured of a high post in the government."

"Who is the Radical Party putting their man against?" asked Jean.

"Fernand Clerc."

"One of the land owners." replied Monique.

"Fernand Clerc?" exclaimed Andre. "I had supper with him last night at the Hayot plantation."

"Did he give you a speech about his politics?" asked Monique.

"Not a thing," replied Andre. "What are his politics?"

"To rid the island of all the taverns, prostitutes and liquor," replied Jean. "That's why I didn't except the invitation to attend the supper at the Hayots last night. Clerc and I get into nasty arguments about his issues. He thinks this island is the biblical Sodom."

"I never thought of him as being like that," said Andre.

Jean turned to Monique and said, "To be fair, you must tell Andre about the senator's views about the sins of St. Pierre."

"You mean he's a bible thumper?" asked Andre.

"No, he doesn't expound that much reformation like Clerc. He just feels that there should be more control over the vices. We have a bad venereal problem here, especially in the mulatto quarter." answered Monique.

"What party does Clerc represent?" asked Andre.

"The Progressive Party," answered Monique.

"Clerc seems to have lost many of his following," said Jean. "His speeches bear marks of uncertainty and he seems to be deviating further and further from the Progressive Party ticket."

"In fact, his articles in the paper seem to be fairly vicious lately," said Monique "They seem to be uniting the Radical Party by hardening the resolve of the coloured voters to drive white bigotry from office."

"Although," said Jean "in many ways, both parties have hinged on single issues such as better education and better working hours for non-whites."

"That's true," replied Monique, "but only on those issues because both parties realize that they are good selling points to the non-whites on the island."

Andre looked at his watch and turned to Jean and said, "It looks like I must leave and pick up Rachelle at the orphanage."

"I will take you there, Andre," said Jean.

"No No! It's OK, I will find my way." replied Andre. "You stay here and enjoy yourself."

"It's been nice seeing you Andre," said Monique. "I hope we will meet again."

"I certainly hope so, Monique," and with that, Andre left the table. He waved at Jean and slipped out of the tavern and into the night. He wound his way up the streets until he located the orphanage where Rachelle was waiting for him at the entrance.

"Andre!" she called out to him. "There is someone here to see you."

A man came out of the shadows and introduced himself to Andre. "I am the chief warden at the military prison."

"Yes?" asked Andre "What can I do for you?"

"We have a man who is very ill and requires immediate attention."

"Very well," said Andre, "I will come." then he turned to Rachelle.

"You don't mind do you, dear?"

"No, Andre," she replied "I will come with you and wait in the chief warden's office

The three of them climbed into Rachelle's carriage which had been sent from the Hayot plantation to meet her. In less than half an hour, they were on the other side of St. Pierre when the massive grey walls of the prison loomed in front of them.

The chief warden took them inside the main gate of the prison and in minutes they were in his office.

He looked at Rachelle and said, "If the young lady doesn't mind, the doctor and I will leave her in my office while we attend to the prisoner."

"That will be fine," replied Rachelle. "I'll wait here for your return."

The two men left the office and walked across the main yard and into another building. After climbing down some stairs, they reached a dark passageway, lit only by a small lantern. They turned a corner and met one of the guards standing outside one of the cells.

"How is he?" asked the chief warden.

"Still groaning but seems to be breathing alright now," replied the guard.

"He got a bit smart with us and I am afraid the guards got a little out of hand in dealing with him," said the chief warden as he turned to face Andre.

The cell door was opened and the lantern was handed to Andre who then entered the cell. He was struck by the stench and dampness of the cell which was only six feet by six. On the floor was the prisoner, curled up in a little ball in a feeble attempt to retain his body heat. As Andre placed the lamp beside the prostrate form, he was aghast at what he saw. The man's face had been beaten, the skin of his face, puffed up. His eyes were bloodshot and his mouth was bleeding where several of his teeth were knocked out. He was a black man and appeared to be in his late teens.

Andre got the guard to assist him in lifting the man onto his straw sack. When that was done, Andre placed his ear to the man's chest.

"I suggest that you don't beat this man anymore unless you want to kill him," said Andre in a surly manner.

"He will be dying on the eighth of this month anyhow," replied the chief warden.

"I don't understand," said Andre

"This pig raped a white woman and for that he will hang on Thursday."

"Well I will repeat what I said.' continued Andre as he examined the unconscious body on the mat. "If you want this man to be alive by Thursday, I am telling you to stop beating him. From the looks of things, it appears that he has received more than one beating."

"Yes, that's true," said the chief warden. "The first night we placed him in the condemned cell, some trusties opened his door and beat him with wooden stakes."

Andre did what he could, which wasn't much, but after being assured that more blankets would be given to the prisoner, Andre left the cell and waited for the cell door to be closed before he spoke.

"I always thought that the guillotine was the method of execution in the colonies."

We haven't used the guillotine for many years doctor," replied the chief warden. "We found that the wood would seize up with the dampness and the blade would occasionally stick. We now use the gallows." Andre flinched at the word 'gallows'

The two men walked through the passageway and Andre gave a sigh of relief as he breathed the air outside while walking through the main yard even though the air had a sharp sulfuric smell to it. A few minutes later he and Rachelle were escorted out of the prison. Andre spoke very little on the way to the Hayot plantation as he thought of that poor man in the darkened cell, beaten, cold and with only six days to live.

"Andre!" said Rachelle, "I thought I was going to be able to have tomorrow off from the orphanage but it seems that a number of the children have been very ill and I have been asked to go to work tomorrow to help the staff." She squirmed when she said this to Andre and flinched when she saw the expression on his face change from disappointment to one of anger.

"I can appreciate your problem Rachelle but do you understand mine?"

"I am not sure I understand what you mean, Andre," replied Monique.

"I traveled all the way to Martinique from France to marry you but you seem to be too busy doing other things. We never really get to see and know one another."

"But Andre, surely you can understand my situation. I have been working at the orphanage for the past year and all of a sudden a number of the children get sick. Do you want me to drop everything?"

"You will have to drop everything on the eighth when we take the *Romania* back to France," said Andre rather firmly.

"I realize that, Andre but until then, please let me ease off my work load and social commitments."

"Rachelle!" said Andre. "Do you love me?"

"Of course!"

"Then you will have to spend more time with me than you are right now."

Rachelle didn't answer, so the two rode in silence; both with their own thoughts. Later that night, they got into an argument about where her real love lies; in Paris with Andre or in St. Pierre with the orphans.

Chapter Eight

The early morning sun was just rising behind Pelee, tinting its peak a reddish brown when the priest of Le Prechure looked outside of the Town Hall compound. He looked at the guard approaching him and said, "Will you fetch the garrison commander and tell him that the villagers have decided to return to Prechure?"

"But," stammered the guard, "You can't leave here. That is the order from the governor."

"Just go fetch the commander!" the priest said angrily.

The guard left his post and ran up the street to locate the commander. As soon as he left, the priest entered the compound and watched and listened to his people as they prepared for their journey home. The adults moved about quickly while the children danced and laughed. Then the priest gave the signal and swiftly the villagers slipped out of the compound and moved up Rue Victor Hugo.

Few of them had slept that night after having been herded into the confines of the compound. The night had been warm and sticky. Through the hours of darkness, they discussed and argued their plans and finally decided that it would be better to live in their own village then remain in the compound.

The soldier found the duty officer and told him of the villager's desire to return to Le Prechure. The duty officer told the soldier that the garrison commander wouldn't be awake for two more hours and to tell them to wait till then. When the soldier returned, he found an empty compound.

Andre woke up early and, realizing that Rachelle would be going to the orphanage with the carriage, he decided to accompany her and spend the day in the city.

As they were driving down the hill, they saw the villagers marching out of the city so Andre decided to go with them to see if he could be of any help on their journey to Le Prechure.

Rachelle dropped him off just ahead of the column and continued her own journey to the orphanage. They had agreed to meet for supper that evening.

"Good morning, Father!" Andre called out to the priest."

"Good morning yourself, Doctor," replied the priest. "I trust you had a pleasant evening."

"Yes, thank you," replied Andre. "Where did you all sleep last night?"

"In the Town Hall compound however we have decided to return back to our village."

"Isn't there still the danger of lava flowing into your village?"

"I don't know but we want to see for ourselves as to what the situation is there." replied the priest.

"I hope you will let me accompany you to your village."

"Yes, of course, my son." replied the priest.

As the villagers trekked towards their village along the twisting road that followed the coastline of that part of Martinique, freshly dug mounds were on both sides of the road. There the animals that had choked under the ash fall were buried.

Andre looked to his right across the hill leading up toward the massive Pelee, silhouetted against the morning sun, and wondered what the mountain had in store for them that day.

Then he heard the singing voices of the villagers and wondered if the priest felt like Moses, leading his people out of Egypt.

By midday, even the most optimistic of the villagers had come to the conclusion that it would probably be impossible to reach the village, at least for another day. The reason was obvious. When they had reached the Blanche River, the stream they had easily forded the previous day was now cascading down the mountain with mud, boulders and debris racing toward the sea. Its banks were no longer definable near the coast since at the mouth, the water had spread itself over a quarter of a mile of ground.

The priest led them further up the mountain in hopes that the river might be narrow enough, but the higher they climbed, the faster the water flowed until it seemed to be boiling as it flowed down the slopes of Pelee.

For an hour, the villagers sat near the river debating what they should do. Some where in favor of returning to the compound in St. Pierre; others said it would be better to seek refuge at the Convent of the Notre Dame at Morne Rouge. It was finally decided that they would trek inland and go to Morne Rouge.

They had gone about a kilometre when they heard a dull roar from the side of the mountain.

Andre looked up and saw an avalanche of mud rushing down the mountain towards them. As it traveled, it folded back on itself, rearing to form a wall of boiling mass in which were embedded rocks and trees.

The villagers stood transfixed at what they saw, mutely disbelieving what their eyes were seeing. The tremors caused by Pelee, shook the ground so violently that it bowled over the villagers like bowling pins. In panic, they scattered in all directions. The priest called out to them to follow him and soon the villagers were running after the priest towards St. Pierre. Just as the last of the villagers ran from the path of the avalanche, the roaring mass rushed past them, sweeping away the forest before it. A few minutes later the villagers stared at the plain of mud that had cut the forest clean for a quarter of a kilometre in width.

They realized that it had also cut off their route to Morne Rouge and to get to safety, they would have to return to St. Pierre.

By midday, they reached the city only to find that the city had increased its population by hundreds. The newcomers; all from the hamlets outside of the city had fled to the city during the tremor and were now roaming the streets, blocking pedestrian and carriage traffic, disrupting commercial life, and creating a general nuisance of themselves in the cafes and restaurants. Many of the people told of crops being blighted and of their houses filled with dust.

When the villagers of Le Prechure reached the Roxelane River Bridge they looked with horror at the raging river beneath it. The muddy waters, choked with trees, were causing another source of concern. On closer examination, bodies of animals and humans were seen floating down the churning water on their journey out to the sea.

All morning, August Ciparis, the condemned man in the military prison, stood on tip toe to peer through the narrow slit that allowed light into his cell. The opening was 15 centimetres high and 30 centimetres long. Four stubby bars were set in the gap and were now giving Ciparis a handhold to support himself as he peered into the yard.

Every morning at dawn, he had watched the trusties, mulattos; all of them scuffle across the yard to the other side of the prison where their cell block was. Then they would unlock the cells of their fellow prisoners for roll call.

The prison at St. Pierre, like so many other prisons in other French colonies, was run by the prisoners. The administrative personnel were kept to a minimum. The routine discipline in the cell blocks, the running of the kitchens and hospital and the detailing of work parties were always handled by the prison trusties. At night when the prison gates were locked, the prison was under the care of the prison trusties with the exception of the guards at the gates. This system was always a convenience to the prison administration but the prisoners always suffered abuses because of it. It was here in the no man's land of society that corruption, bribery and death were commonplace. In St. Pierre, the trusties had a deep hatred for negroes which comprised the bulk of the prison population.

Ciparis, only nineteen when sentenced to death, was the trustee's most hated prisoner because he had been convicted of raping a woman, a white woman. His first night in the condemned cell was one of terror. The trusties armed with Wooden stakes, rushed at him after opening his cell door. They left him half dead from the beating and every night since then, he had received similar beatings although the beatings stopped after the visit from the doctor.

He watched the prisoners stack the lumber beside the prison wall. This was the lumber that was going to be used for the scaffold from which he was to hang. All morning he watched as a number of prisoners erected the scaffold. When the two posts had been erected, the noonday whistle blew, and the gallows party left their work to partake of the noon meal.

Suddenly Ciparis felt the ground shake below his feet and he watched with a slight twinge of amusement as the gallows crashed to the ground. Perhaps it was a hopeful sign for the future.

Later in the afternoon, Andre went to the park in the centre of the city to bask in the warm sun. He had been sitting on a bench for only half an hour when he noticed a familiar figure approaching the park. It was Monique Rouseau.

Andre left the bench and greeted her, "Monique, it's nice to see you again."

"Hello Andre," replied Monique. "It's nice to see you, too."

"What brings you to the park today?"

"Oh, I always come here when I get a chance."

"Would you like to sit with me?" asked Andre as he pointed to the bench.

"Delighted," answered Monique.

The two sat on a bench and Andre asked, "Have you seen Jean today?"

"No." replied Monique. "I only see him once in a while, especially since he has to run the plantation since his father's death."

"I certainly have had an active time since I came to this island a couple of days ago."

"Oh?" asked Monique. "What happened today?"

Andre commenced to tell Monique about the villagers attempting to return to their village and the subsequent avalanches.

"I am afraid we are in for more from Pelee than just avalanches," remarked Monique as she turned her head towards Pelee.

Andre stared at Monique's face as she spoke, wishing that Rachel's face had the same beauty.

All afternoon Andre and Monique talked; Andre about Paris and Monique about St. Pierre. At six, Andre realized that he had to pick up Rachelle and said to Monique, "I will have to excuse myself as I have to pick up my fiancé at the orphanage."

"I understand." said Monique. "If you two find yourselves down in the mulatto quarter, I hope you will come over to the Radical Party headquarters and listen to Senator Knight speak."

"Thanks for the invitation." answered Andre as he left the bench and waved goodbye to Monique.

He walked to the orphanage and met Rachelle who was inside eating with the other staff.

"I thought we were going to have supper together tonight." said Andre rather angrily.

"I am sorry Andre," said Rachelle. "The situation is very serious here and I have to remain in the orphanage for the rest of the evening."

"Very well, remain!" said Andre in a huff as he turned and stomped out of the room.

Rachelle followed him to the entrance to the orphanage and said, "I really am sorry, Andre. We could drive home again at midnight."

Andre turned and asked "Do you want me to look at the children?"

"No, I mean, we have had a doctor look at them and he says they will be alright in a few days!"

"Very well." said Andre as he walked passed the gate leading to the street. Andre half expected this turn of events and angrily walked down the street, not even looking back at Rachelle as she called to him to remind him about going home with her later.

In less than an hour, Andre was in the narrow building that housed the headquarters of the Radical Party. He couldn't find Monique in the crowd and was about to leave when he heard a voice call out his name. He turned and saw a tall black man approaching him. He appeared to be in his sixties and was clean shaven but had white hair.

"Young man," the black man called out again. "I trust you are Doctor Verlaine?"

"Yes, that is so. And who are you Sir?"

"I am Amedee Knight," was the reply.

"How did you know who I was, Senator?"

"I saw you leave the park earlier and Monique told me who you were."

"Speaking of Monique, where is she?"

"Oh, she will be back shortly. Why don't you stay and wait for her?"

A man approached Andre and the Senator and said, "We are ready Senator."

"Thank you, I will be right there." the Senator said in return. "I must give my fiery speech, Andre. I'm sure Monique will be back shortly."

"I'll wait for her, Sir."

Senator Knight followed the man to the dais and as soon as he reached it, he began to speak. "Pelee has given us a sign. Its smoke and fire has brought the party together and united us. The mountain will only sleep when the whites are no longer in power. The white business houses and stores must show more Christian tolerance to their black brothers."

A loud cheer went up and then the Senator continued. "You have asked me as to who I wish to support in our party. Without hesitation, I support Percin."

Another cheer went up and again the hand of the Senator went up. "Lagrosillere will not be forgotten. He will still have a place and position."

Someone tapped Andre on the shoulder and when he turned, he was looking into the face of Monique, beaming with smiles. "I'm glad you could come to the rally." Then she looked about her and asked, "Where is Rachelle?"

"She's still at the orphanage. She says she has to stay at the orphanage to work with the sick children."

"I'm sorry to hear that."

"Well, perhaps you might show me some of the customs of your people."

"Then you are in time to watch one of our funerals."

"Someone you know?"

"Yes, a friend I knew since I was a child." Then Monique led Andre outside. "We have to go to the military hospital where my friend's body will be picked up."

"What's her name?"

"It's a man and his name was Eli Victor."

The two of them walked up the Victor Hugo and finally arrived at the hospital where a large crowd had gathered.

"He died this afternoon after a brief illness in the hospital, so we are taking him with us to bury him," said Monique.

Just then the crowd made way for some of the mourners coming out of the hospital. The body of the deceased was carried out on a crude stretcher made from sacking and two bamboo poles.

"Poor Eli," lamented Monique. "He had been poor all his life as he is now in death. No hearse or coffin, just sacking and bamboo poles."

"And all his friends to bade him fare well," added Andre. "He certainly died rich."

Monique looked at Andre and saw another part of him she didn't know he had, being white. It was human understanding.

"When I think of Eli walking with bare feet all his life, I think of him as being poor. But now that you mention it, I realize that he really was rich and had been all his life. He was surrounded by friends all of his life."

The funeral party walked slowly, as befitting a ritual dedicated to appeasing the departed soul of Eli Victor so that it would not haunt the living.

It was a ritual known as the 'Nine Nights.' Its roots lay in worshiping their ancients and worshiping Voodooism. Among the upper classes it had degenerated into something like a wake. The nine days and nights after death were used to bring succor to the bereaved relatives. But to the poor people, the bare feet people in the mulatto quarter, the ritual meant more; in the case of Eli Victor, it meant sending his soul to heaven.

In the darkness, the pall bearers set off, singing softly among themselves. Andre and Monique followed close behind.

A large crowd had gathered on the far side of the Pont Basin, at an iron-girdered bridge that crossed over the Roxelane River that led into the mulatto quarter. The crowd was the main mourning party for Eli Victor. In the distance they could hear the distant singing of the funeral chant. In another moment, the singing was loud in their ears. Someone struck a match and tiny flames flared, and soon the torches everyone was carrying flared into life, casting long shadows as they each sputtered to life.

Soon the waiting crowd began to sing in answer to the singers who were approaching. At last the pall-bearing party came into sight, rounding a bend in the road, then the singing of both crowds became as one.

The crowd began its march across the bridge to merge with the approaching party. Fresh shoulders eagerly took up the burden of Eli Victor's body then singing as they went, they began to cross the bridge. Barefoot, the mourners trod softly through the ash mud. Eli Victor was carried in their midst like the body of a Pharaoh.

By then, Andre and Monique were about twenty metres from the main party when the tremors came. They looked up at Pelee and the ever increasing red sky above it. Then they heard the screams of the men and women and children on the bridge and felt the surge and press of the crowd as the crowd backed away from the bridge. A new tremor, more violent than the first, wrenched the iron bridge from its concrete supports and twisted the bridge like a pretzel. Thirty men, women and children including the corpse of Eli Victor and his widow, were pitched into the raging water below and were being swept out to sea.

The glow from the lava in the throat of the volcano reflected from the clouds overhanging the volcano coloured the rock around the rim a dull red. In a few minutes a thin sliver of bright orange lava poured from the crater and began to move slowly down the mountain. It was descending on the northern slope of the volcano out of sight of St. Pierre, although the subsequent fires in the forest could be seen by everyone in the city. Much to everyone's surprise, there was no noise coming from the volcano, just the occasional twitch and the unseen lava stream burning its way through the jungle, its fire reflecting off the leaves of the trees.

The initial tremors that had destroyed the iron-girder bridge had confined itself to the mulatto quarter. There the people were in considerable fear for their lives. Clocks had stopped, floors had tilted, glass windows shattered and doors had opened. Crockery and plaster fell to the floor.

By the time the panic had subsided, eight other people had died. Five of them had been struck by pieces of falling masonry. Three children were crushed on the waterfront beneath a stack of rum barrels which had been toppled over by the tremor and rolled over them.

News of the tremors and deaths traveled to several parts of St. Pierre and instead of creating panic, the news provoked a strange calm. People from different parts of the city began to make their way to the mulatto quarter to see the damage and to hear first account experiences from the survivors.

When Andre and Monique got to the centre of the mulato quarter, the streets were filled with an influx of people, many from the outskirts seeking shelter and reassurance. In an hour, the area around the Cathedral was a seething mass. Troops were attempting to clear the area.

The population of St. Pierre had by now swollen to thirty thousand. Not only was food scarce, there was also a shortage of water. The drinking water was polluted by the ash falls and animals were dying in the streets. The situation was deteriorating steadily. Little children wandered the streets aimlessly, their bodies covered with ash. The animals and birds still dying in the streets, made a pitiful sound, adding to the voices of confusion of the children.

Suddenly there a series of loud explosions heard from the vicinity of Pelee. Andre along with everyone else looked at Pelee and saw the glowing red cone become hidden by an enormous black cloud of smoke. The sky darkened around the area of the volcano but shortly after that, the area of the crater was traversed by flashes of lightning. The rumbling from inside the volcano grew louder until no one could hear another speaking.

Anarchy was beginning to reign over St. Pierre. Several food and vegetable shops were looted and soldiers were called to evict people from a number of hotels and cafes where they had demanded lodging and food. Fights broke out between refugees from the country side and local residents who refused to open up their homes as sanctuaries.

The heat from the mouth of the crater created so much condensation above it that rain came down on the mountain in torrents. All the streams quickly flooded until they cascaded down the mountain like mighty rivers. Many of the streams rushed into the Roxelane River until a huge wall of water was built up at the midpoint between its source and the sea. In minutes, a wave of tidal proportions came roaring down the Roxeland River, gathering more water as it approached the city. By the time it rushed through St. Pierre it was five metres high. It rushed over a bridge, completely submerging it and those crossing it. By the time it had passed, the bridge and those it carried had disappeared in the water that smashed into them. The wave continued on its journey until it reached the power plant which supplied most of the city with its electrical power. The wave smashed into the building, caving in the walls and burying everything under tons of water and debris. The wave, partly spent by the impact of the power plant roared out to sea, carrying with it, trees, boulders, bodies of both humans and animals. While the wave was rushing through its destructive route, the volcano continued to roar and the ground shook.

Fighting was everywhere, and it wasn't long before Andre and Monique were in the midst of it.

"Andre!" screamed Monique, "Quickly! Let's get to my house! We will be safe there."

Andre yelled his approval of her plan and together, they shoved, elbowed and pushed their way through the fighting mob.

The streets were much darker since the electricity was no longer available and it was only by the occasional flashes of lightning and the flames that poked through the heavy black smoke, that anyone could see where they were going.

The black cloud descended over the city like a thick fog, choking everyone it reached, bringing tears to their eyes and temporarily blinding them.

Monique led Andre by the hand as she groped along the street, her hand reaching for familiar land marks such as neighbour's gates and doors.

"We are nearly there!" gasped Monique.

Behind them they could hear the screaming of the townspeople as they tried to get indoors to escape the pall of suffocating smoke and ash that was choking them.

Then from the area of Pelee, came another thunderous roar. Andre glanced behind him and through his partially opened eyes; he saw flashes of red light through the dense smoke. Mt. Pelee began coughing up red hot boulders, some weighing more than half a tonne each. They arched through the air, and landed on the countryside below. Some of the huge flaming boulders rolled through the forests, cane fields and hamlets, setting everything they touched afire.

"We're here!" gasped Monique as she pulled Andre into her house.

"Thank God!" answered Andre.

Monique let go of his hand and began fumbling for a lantern. She lit it and the room began to light up. As soon as she placed the lantern on the table, Monique began to gather up a sheet and stuffed it under the crack in her door.

"I hope that will keep the smoke out," she said.

"I feel sorry for those poor devils outside choking in that damned smoke." added Andre.

"Well perhaps it will be over soon."

Monique busied herself trying to seal the house with clothes and sheets in hopes that the deadly smoke and ash would keep out of the two room house. When she had finally finished, she perked her ears and heard the voices of people running down the street. The screams were pitiful, dying screams. The ash was clogging their lungs as they inhaled it. The moisture in the air coupled with the fine volcanic dust caked the inside of their lungs like wet cement.

"Let us in! Let us in!" they cried. The victims banged on the doors of the houses trying to escape the killer smoke and ash.

Soon they were banging on Monique's door but she didn't dare open the door. Together Andre and Monique braced themselves against the door in hopes of keeping it firm against the continuous onslaught. They both realized that if they opened the door, they would be doomed also. Soon, the crowd left and vented their fury on the door of the next house.

Monique went to the other room and called to Andre. "Come in here, Andre. We will be safe from the smoke in here."

Andre left the front room and went into the other one and saw Monique sitting on her bed.

"It won't be safe for you to return to the Hayot Plantation tonight Andre so you may spend the night here if you wish."

"But I have to take Rachelle home."

"If she has any sense at all, Andre, she will be spending the night in the orphanage."

"Yes, I suppose you are right."

"Andre, you don't have to feel ashamed sleeping here."

Andre reached over and picked up Monique's hand and kissed it and said "I'm not ashamed. I am extremely grateful to you for letting me spend the night here."

Monique leaned over to Andre and kissed him on his cheek and said, " We won't play those silly games as to who will sleep on the bed and who will sleep on the floor, will we?"

"I will sleep on the floor, Monique. It's your house."

"You can sleep on the bed with me Andre."

"No! No! I can't do that."

"Sleeping with a mulatto would disgust you?"

"Monique," said Andre softly. "There is nothing I would like better than to sleep with you. It's just that I wouldn't want to offend you."

Monique moved towards Andre and slowly began to unbutton his shirt. When the buttons were undone, she peeled off his shirt and admired his heaving chest. Andre felt a tingling sensation as she began undoing the buttons of his trousers. As she was stripping him, he began slipping her blouse smoothly over her silk-like skin to reveal her well-shaped breasts. They both sat on the edge of her bed, while each was stripping the other. Andre had seen naked women before but never like the magnificent body that sat next to him. He had even slept with naked women before but Monique was beyond his previous encounters.

As they lay down together, Andre slid his hands over her naked body; first her breasts and then her ass and finally her crotch. She responded by guiding his penis into her crotch and then lying on top of him so that she could dictate the rhythm. Her rhythmic gyrations were no different than what she had done earlier on the dance floor. Only now, instead of having to settle with only his imagination, as experienced by the hundreds of others who watched her on the dance floor, Andre was experiencing the culmination of their erotic fantasizing, not to mention his own.

As Andre plunged deeper and deeper into Monique's body, she squirmed, her hips gyrating while her soft hands squeezed the cheeks of his ass. He was in heaven, a heaven he had never experienced before, let alone entered. Back in the recesses of his mind, he wondered if his future wife would be a purgatory in bed compared to Monique. Before his mind dwelled on that any further, Monique whispered, "Now let me show you what else I can do for you."

For the rest of the night, and into the early hours of the morning, Monique showed Andre what one human body can do for another. Andre was passing through the Gates of Heaven.

Chapter Nine

It was about 12:30 in the early morning when the volcano roared back to life. The thunderous roar was heard as far away as Fort du France, 24 kilometres to the west. Andre, in an instant, was pulled from the caresses of Heaven and plummeted into the depths of Hell.

He and Monique jumped out of bed in unison and ran to the window. Monique opened the shutters and both stared disbelievingly at Pelee. It was like standing on the brink of Hell. Every few seconds, flashes of lightning of blinding intensity lit up the black and purple clouds which hung over the volcano. Between the flashes, bursts of flame shot out of the crater; their brilliant orange lightning up the countryside. Every few seconds, scintillating stars burst forth like crackling fireworks and winding in and out of this spectacle were whirling lines of tornado-like flames. Throughout this fanfare of light, the mountain roared and the ground shook.

What had previously been a city of gloom and panic was now the opposite. A great many of the people were out in the street whooping it up as they watched the display of celestial fireworks. Gone was the killer fog which had suffocated thirty persons in the street and in its place was a clear night lit up with the colour of the white buildings reflecting the fire from Pelee as it fluctuated between shades of orange and red. Down in the streets, the children, now fully awake, raced around the streets, sending small swirls of ash eddying into the air from their scurrying feet.

After a few minutes had elapsed, a great pattering of pumice fell upon the town, and for a while, it sounded like a tropical hailstorm.

Some of the fragments were a centimetre or so in size, others as fine as sand. But even the smallest particles came down with such force that it stung the skin of everyone that hadn't got indoors in time. The ash fall lasted ten minutes and during that time, the streets were deserted.

Monique closed the shutters, drew the curtains and headed towards the bed. Andre followed and within a minute, both were in each other's embrace again.

A number of kilometres to the northeast of them, on the other side of Pelee, the villagers of Ajoupa-Bouillon had gathered in their village square to watch the display from Pelee. They had watched in utter fear as the red hot boulders shot out of the crater and cascade down the slopes of the volcano towards their village.

There was some concern by a number of the villagers that perhaps it would be best to leave the village and seek shelter in the city but others counseled otherwise. It was finally decided by the majority with the insistence of the village mayor, Bernark Kloss, that the village was safe from destruction as most of boulders shooting out of the crater headed towards St. Pierre and that the fireworks were as harmless as that and nothing more. Soon, everyone returned to their homes and in less than half an hour, every light in the village was out and the village streets and houses were only lit up in a reddish hue from the reflection of the red clouds in the sky.

During the early hours of the morning, immense pressures built up inside Pelee. For the past week, it had been producing seismic vibrations which are characteristic of other volcanoes in the Antilles. These are small localized earth tremors of varying intensity. Pelee, like many of the other volcanoes in the Caribbean chain, had a thin crust of rock on its outside which did not meet the deep-rooted strains rising from several thousand metres below.

The rocks were ground together under immense pressure, liquefying to temperatures of over 4,000 degrees. The white-hot mass of molten lava steadily forced its way to the surface and in most cases, the hot mass escaped to the crater of the volcano. Unfortunately, some of the white hot mass found its way through a weak fissure to a spot just under the village of Ajoupa-Bouillon. Just before dawn, the fissure weakened and with a terrifying roar, the white hot lava escaped through the ground.

The zone of destruction began a short distance below the village church and extended through the village and a quarter of a kilometre down the slope of Pelee.

The blast destroyed all it touched and in a matter of seconds, the lush vegetation had burned into an arid wasteland. Cattle and horses caught in the mainstream of the explosion were burned to death, others still alive, had their hides burned off and were writhing on the ground, the raw flesh exposed to the morning air and insects.

The hot lava burst through a number of homes burning their wooden frames and instantly killing the occupants. For those who weren't killed instantly, their fate was far worse. They had to live with their hideous burns albeit only for a short time before they expired.

It was Monique who heard the knocking on her door. She left the warm confines of her bed where Andre was sprawled.

"Hello. Is anyone in?" asked the voice on the other side of the door.

"Who is it?" asked Monique.

"Jean. Jean Aubrey." replied the voice apprehensively.

Monique put on a house coat and opened the door.

"Come in Jean." said Monique with a smile.

"I've come to fetch Andre Verlain."

"What makes you think he's here?" said Jean angrily.

"If you want Andre to spend the night with you, that's your affair but right now he is needed. All the doctors are needed."

"Why." asked Monique. "What's happened?"

"There has been a volcanic explosion under Ajoupa- Boullion."

"Oh no!" exclaimed Monique.

Monique ran over to the bed and woke Andre up.

"Andre, Andre" she called. "You must get up. Jean Aubrey is here."

"So what?" answered Andre in a sarcastic tone of voice.

"You're needed in Ajoupa-Boullion"

"Why?" asked Andre sleepily.

Jean stepped into the room and answered the question, then followed it with an order "Get up! You're needed now."

Andre quickly dressed and after a short talk with Monique he followed Jean outside where a carriage waited for the both of them.

Before long the two of were racing across the city and heading into the hinterland towards the stricken village.

"Do you know if Rachelle got home safely last night?" asked Andre.

"Why should you care?" Jean asked angrily. "After all, you were spending the night with Monique."

"Who I sleep with is none of your business, Jean, so don't bring it up again!" retorted Andre in a high pitched voice.

"I will bring it up again and I'll tell you why." Jean paused and then continued. "Before Rachelle went to Paris and met you, I was semi-engaged to her. Then she fell in love with you so I found Monique. Now I find that you are not content with taking Rachelle from me, you want to sleep with my other choice also."

Andre looked at Jean and said quietly, "I am sorry Jean. I really didn't know you were serious with Monique."

"I am not serious about her. I would never marry a mulatto but I think of her as my mistress."

"You mean," gasped Andre, you were thinking of her as a mistress?" Then he continued. "That is getting pretty low."

"When you slept with Monique last night, were you thinking of Monique or were you thinking of Rachelle?"

At this part of the conversation, Andre was at a complete loss for words. The two men drove on without a word. They had said enough to each other and nothing further had to be said. Andre just hoped that Jean would keep what he had learned, to himself.

By the time they arrived at the stricken village, a number of the rescuers had arrived along with a few of the doctors from St. Pierre.

The village mayor led the rescuers down the main street. The first houses that he led them to had simply exploded off the face of the slope; even their foundations had disappeared. Further down the street, they came to a small cottage which at the outset had appeared untouched by the blast. But when the rescuers approached it, they could hear a low moaning from inside. One look inside told the story. The occupants had been terribly burned by a jet of steam which had roared up through their floor. The men tenderly lifted the occupants outside while the victims called for water. No sooner had the water been brought to them, they died. The steam and mud, ejected at the velocity of a high pressure hose inflicted unbelievable injuries on the victims. The rescuers knew that there was no way that any of them could have been saved.

In one of the homes, a woman rolled in agony in a corner of her bedroom, her flesh burned and hanging from her bones. The steam had gouged out both her eyes and boiling water had removed the flesh off one of her legs right to the bone.

From house to house, the rescuers went, most vomiting at the sight that was too shattering to comprehend. It was the same, house after house, in some cases, the sightless crying out for help, others writhing in pain, their flesh baked and steamed.

In some cases, the mere handling of the victims was enough to make them scream as their flesh would slide from their bones. The odor from the burned bodies and flesh was sickening.

It was well into the morning when the rescuers were able to assess the damage and loss of life. There were 158 dead and 30 died. Never before had Andre seen such horror.

Several kilometres away, near the coast, just west of the volcano, a large number of cane cutters were working in Doctor Guerin's cane fields. Sunday was not a working day for the mulattos but for some reason, the Doctor had ordered them to work. To refuse meant dismissal which not only meant loss of income and free living accommodations but also a virtual impossibility of employment anywhere else on the island. In essence, they were his slaves.

Through a gap in the middle of the cane, Doctor Guerin, seated on his grey stallion, watched the long double rank of workers moving steadily forward, leveling the tall cane as they moved up the slope while singing, accompanied by a drummer boy who kept abreast of them. The men worked in pairs, each pair twenty metres from the next. Each man carried a machete, nearly a metre long and curved like a buccaneers cutlass. The cane cutters wielded the machetes close to the ground, the tall stalks falling to the ground. A few yards behind each pair of men came a woman, whose task it was together up the stalks of cane and bind them into bundles.

Suddenly there was a series of screams from the cane field and Doctor Guerin turned and galloped towards the source of the screams.

By the time he reached the area, it was too late for him to do anything. The earth had suddenly split open and swallowed twenty men and woman into the opening; then freakishly the gap had closed crushing the cane cutters and their women to death.

The surviving workers without waiting to free the bodies of their fellow workers, scattered in all directions to their homes.

A finger of smoke rose several hundred metres into the air from the summit of Pelee. For a while, it hung there black and straight. Then, under pressure from inside the crater, the strand of smoke began to curl on itself, flattening out at the top to form a small cloud. Then the cloud wavered, and was dispersed by the wind currents raging around the summit of the volcano. Soon after, a fresh cloud of smoke left the crater. Gathering speed every second, the cloud started to spread over the sky like a huge fan. The cloud suddenly rose upwards of nine thousand metres, racing across the sky. A few minutes later the cloud descended and as it did, it disgorged a shower of stones and mud onto the city.

The first fragments of pumice shattered on the streets, sending hot splinters flying in all directions. Many were injured by the splinters and the hot mud which singed the people in the streets. For five minutes, St. Pierre was shrouded in darkness as the fan-like cloud reached across the sky until only a sliver of light appeared on the horizon.

The tolling bells of the Cathedral woke Ciparis at midday and as he peered out of his cell window, he thought that by this time next Thursday, he would be hanging by his neck out in the yard. He knew that this would be the last time he would hear the bells because when they ring on Ascension Day, Thursday, the executioner will have done his dirty deed.

For some time Ciapris knew that the prison in St. Pierre was one of a few that still retained the gibbet for executions. In Metropolitan France, the guillotine invented by Dr. Guillotine had come into wide use. Ironically, the inventor was one of the first men to die by his own invention. The guillotine had replaced the firing squad which in the martial spirit of the new Republic had come into use as the accepted mode of execution. The firing squad had found disfavor in Martinique simply because there was a shortage of skilled marksmen on the island. The guillotine, despite its reputation of being precise and swift, had disadvantages in the tropics. Aside from the fact that the blade and framework warping in the warm climate, would produce 'terrible consequences' as one report put it, the uprights if not checked with a plumb line to see that they were perfectly vertical, would slow the descent of the blade, sometimes cutting only part way into the victims neck. This would be distressing-not least, presumably to the condemned man.

Although most prisons in France had relaxed their discipline over the years and were thinking more towards treatment rather than punishment, the military prison is St. Pierre was one where they believed in the old school. Sunday, which was considered a day of rest was generally considered a hard day because with exception of their meal times, the prisoners would have to remain in their cells.

Since breakfast, the prison was unusually quiet. Ciparis looked outside and although he couldn't see the top of the volcano, he knew that the crater was hurling out wild sheets of yellow cloud. As it was, Pelee's top was being lashed in fury by the smoke and was soon buried in the dark shadows of the smoke. Oddly enough, there was a complete absence of noise which made it seem all the more eerie. The clouds came out rolling on top of each other twirling themselves into lofty columns and finally into mushroom caps.

Ciparis could faintly hear mumbling and whispering in the other cells near him and within minutes, the voices increased in volume until the prisoners from all corners of the prison were yelling. They wanted to be transferred to the prison at Fort du France immediately before Pelee wiped them out.

Ciparis could hear the sound of wood splintering against metal as the men tried to break their doors down with their chairs. He watched with interest as a dozen guards marched into the yard and began firing into the windows of the cell blocks.

Monique had decided to call on her friend, Julie Cabou, who lived only a few short blocks away. Later the two women were talking about the events of the last few days.

"You know Julie. I can't believe that Mount Pelee is acting this way. Never in my lifetime have I ever seen the mountain act like this."

"That's true." replied Julie. "Did you see how thick that yellow smoke was this morning?"

"Yes. I sure hope that we are not going to get any more smoke. The air is insufferable as it is with that sulfuric smell."

"Oh. You haven't heard?"

"Heard what?"

Monique paused then spoke, "Ajoupa Boullion had some trouble early this morning. I believe that a fissure burst under the village and that half the town was destroyed. Verlaine and Jean Aubrey went there this morning."

"Speaking of Dr. Verlaine. What's with you two?"

"What have you heard?" asked Monique who was surprised that anyone knew about their relationship.

"Oh, you know." said Julie in a coy manner.

"No, I don't know." replied Monique angrily. "That's why I am asking you."

"Well, you have been seen together—." replied Julie before being cut off by Monique.

"So I have been seen with the man. So what. If I see you talking with that old coot, Doctor Guerin, am I supposed to conclude that you are sleeping with him also?

Julie smiled. Monique had made her point.

Chapter Ten

Within half an hour, the two women had reached the cane field and were joined by some of the workers who had run away when the earth had opened up. By the time they reached the area, some of the bodies had already been dug up.

Julie began clawing at the earth when she realized that her common law husband hadn't been found yet. Her nails scratched at the earth until someone gently pulled her away saying, "We have the shovels now, Julie."

For an hour, the workers dug into the earth and finally all the bodies were uncovered. It would have been better, many thought, had the bodies remained in their makeshift grave. They were horribly crushed beyond recognition.

The prison guards were still firing into the cell blocks in order to quiet the rioting prisoners. Ciparis huddled into a corner as bullets began to enter through the small window and then ricochet off the walls of his cell. After a while, the firing stopped and all that could be heard was the sounds of men crying in pain. There were prisoners hit by the bullets either directly or as a result of the ricochets.

Suddenly Ciparis heard the voice of the prison governor. Ciparis peered out of his cell window and saw a middle-aged fat man standing in the center of the prison yard.

"I will be brief and to the point!" yelled the governor. "Unless this mutiny ceases at once, there will be massive reprisals. I am forthwith rescinding all the privileges from the trusties; all prisoners will be on hard labour from now on and the ring leaders will each receive fifty strokes of the bastinade followed by solitary confinement for one year."

Not a sound was made by the prisoners as none of them wanted to be singled out as ring leaders. Then from a distance, Ciparis heard bolts being drawn from cell doors and men screaming while being dragged out of their cells.

Andre and Jean, accompanied by other men had decided to take a short cut to one of the roads leading to St. Pierre from Ajoupa-Boullion as the main road had become clogged by a landslide. They would warn the military hospital of the pending arrival of the injured being brought from the stricken village.

As they continued on their journey, they picked their way around massive boulders while above them the volcano was pushing out cloud and ash that was descending upon them and partially blinding them.

By early afternoon, the party had emerged upon the lower slope of the volcano and began traversing a long ridge about a thousand metres above sea level. At this point, they had to climb upwards toward the summit and trudge through the thick gray ash. What had been once a green covering of grass was now sulfuric smelling ash, with boulders and pumice rock which had been ejected out of the crater above them. For a moment, they stopped to take a rest and take their bearings.

"You know Andre," said Jean. "I am wondering what you are going to do about Rachelle and Monique."

"I can understand how you feel Andre and I can assure you that I had no intentions of creating hardship upon you."

"Well, I shall have to endure this hardship if you don't make up your mind as to who you are going to take back with you to Paris."

"It's Rachelle. I give you my word." responded Andre.

"Then can I trust you to stay away from Monique?"

"Yes, of course Jean. Here's my hand on it." replied Andre. He knew that that would be a sacrifice because he had hoped to be able to sleep with Monique just one more time so that he could have the Gates of Heaven fixed in his memory but he knew that what he was doing to Rachelle and Jean was wrong so his sacrifice would to some degree be bearable. The two men shook hands then began the trek up the ridge.

Andre looked west from the ridge and saw the blue ocean dashing its waves against the white vertical cliffs of the coastline. In the middle distance, the Blanche River began its course; a muddy flowing sweep of chocolate-cloured water that wound its way down the mountain until it swept past the Cuerin refinery and out to sea. There the muddy water spread out like a large fan into the blue waters of the ocean. Ahead and just above the ridge was a deep ravine which had been cut by the lava of some bygone era.

Jean knew that unless the party retraced their steps and tried to cross Pelee's flank by some other direction, they would have no alternative but to climb the ridge and hope that as higher up the mountain they went, the ravine would be narrow enough for them to cross it.

The first part of the ascent was relatively easy as the ridge offered plenty of foot holds. However as they continued their climb upwards, the weather added to their fears. Andre looked up at the awesome summit which towered above them, gray against the dark clouds in the sky. He watched with fear as the black cloud of ash and debris shot straight upwards into the sky in huge bellows.

Shortly, Pelee's crater became covered with a thick mist that blotted out both the crater and the smoke. The mist descended and soon the entire party was engulfed in the cloud-like substance so that they could only see approximately a hundred metres in any direction. Shortly thereafter, it began to drizzle and the eeriness was heightened by the low rumbling noise deep inside the volcano.

Suddenly a crash of thunder resounded above them and the area was lit up in a white flash of light. They all knew that they were in the crossfire of one of the massive thunder storms that had from time to time struck the top of the mountain. No sooner had the echo of the thunder disappeared into the recesses of the mist when another resounding crash followed, this time even more intense in volume than the last one. And again, the mist took on a bluish tint as the lightning flashed through it.

In a moment, the party was subjected to merciless torrents of rain which peltered them with all the fury that such a storm could muster. Stunned by the force of the storm and soaked to their skins, the men started to slither and slide back the way they had come. What had been a ridge consisting of fairly good footholds was now a steep hill of slippery morass. The rain had washed away the footholds and replaced them with new hollows and fissures in which little streamlets flowed.

Halfway down the mountain, the men felt the ground beneath their feet shake violently and they could hear the rumbling sound from within the bowels of the volcano. Andre knew that when the storm hit them, it was because of the condensation produced by the intense heat coming from the crater of the volcano and he knew that this was just a prelude of what was coming next.

And just as they expected, the red hot lava flow poured out of a crevice in the mountain and began to flow down the slopes. It was only a matter of minutes when Andre heard the sound of steam hissing in the distance, a sound characteristic of rain falling on hot lava.

The men knew they had to run for their lives and occasionally they looked behind them and could see a faint reddish glow through the mist, the mist which intermittently turned white as the lightning flashed through it. Before they had realized it, the men had reached the edge of the ridge which protruded out over the slope like a high cliff. Realizing that there was no way down the cliff, the men turned to face the lava coming towards them. However as the lava approached them it was apparent to them that it would be running down one of the ravines of one of the sides of the ridge. A few minutes of patient waiting proved that had they chosen the ravine on the western side of the ridge to climb down the mountain, they would have ended their lives as ash. With fascination, they watched the red hot lava pour down the ravine and slide past them in its heated fury.

"We have to get out of here, otherwise it's possible that the lava flow way cut us off from the city." yelled one of the men.

"Then," yelled Andre. "We had better climb down the eastern ravine."

"No" retorted one of the men. "We may get trapped in the ravine by the lava flow."

Jean spoke up. "The lava is flowing down the western ravine. We will be OK if we climb down the eastern one."

"I agree." yelled one of the men.

"Not I!" yelled another. He continued. "It's obvious that if the lava flowed down one of the ravines, it could flow down another. I suggest that we stay on the ridge and wait till we see what happens to the eastern ravine."

"That could prove dangerous." yelled Andre. "While we wait, this ravine could be worn away by the lava and crumble into the lava flow with us along with it."

Jean cried out with as much authority his voice could muster. "Those in favor of climbing into the eastern ravine, show their hands."

Half the hands were raised.

"I suppose that we can assume that the rest wish to remain on the ridge," said Jean with a quizzical look in his eye.

"Look. Why don't I run up the ridge a way and see what is coming down the eastern ravine, if anything?" asked Andre.

"That's a good idea," answered one of men.

"OK" said Andre, "I will be back in about five minutes."

Andre left the small party of men, sitting huddled on the edge of the cliff and began his climb up the ridge. After a few minutes of attempting to keep to the thin edge of the ridge he saw a faint reddish glow in the mist at the bottom of the eastern ravine. He waited for another few minutes and saw the lava slowly pouring down the ravine and wondered as to why the lava flow on the western ravine poured down the mountain at a quicker pace than the flow on the other side of the ridge. What ever the reason for the increase in pace, he didn't intend to attempt to ascertain the reason as the heat from both ravines was becoming intolerably unbearable.

Andre began his slippery descent back down the ridge to the others waiting at the cliff and when he reached them, he called out above the roar of the volcano, "We have to take the eastern ravine and now."

"Why. What's wrong?" asked one of the men.

A flash of lightning followed by a clap of thunder interrupted Andre as he was about to speak.

"The lava is starting to come down the eastern ravine also."

"We are trapped." screamed one of the men.

"No. We are not." answered Andre. Then he continued, "The lava is flowing very slowly down the eastern ravine and we can beat it down the mountain.

"I won't go." the man yelled.

"Then stay." answered Andre. "But once you do, you will be stranded here, perhaps for ever."

"We will go down the eastern ravine," called out another of the men.

The men began the dangerous journey back up the ridge. The mud caused by the rain on the ash and earth was slippery beyond all expectations and soon the men were digging their fingers deep into the muck in hopes of securing some form of hold onto the ridge.

Andre heard a shout behind him and turned to see three men begin to slither down the slope of the western ridge.

With terror in their eyes, they looked at the bubbling and boiling lava waiting below and began clawing hopelessly at the slippery morass as it offered no foothold. On closer look, Andre saw that the man nearest the top of the ridge was Jean Aubrey.

"Hang on Jean." called Andre as he climbed towards him.

"I can't. I'm slipping down." cried Jean.

"You must." replied Andre.

Some of the other men tried to reach down to assist the three men but the two men below Jean were beyond any hope of being saved and despite their efforts, they slid down the slope and while clawing at the mud and screaming in agony, the two men slid into the liquid lava and disappeared in two small puffs of smoke.

Andre reached for Jean's hands but just as he was to reach for them Jean grabbed Andre's wrists. Some of the men grabbed Andre's legs and prevented him from being dragged down the slope. Andre felt Jean's muddy hands slip slowly from his wrists and Andre yelled. "Let one of my wrists go so that I can grab your hand."

"I can't." answered Jean. "I will lose the grip on your other wrist."

The two men hung down the side of the ridge for a few minutes, both realizing that in a few short moments, Jean would slip away from Andre for ever.

As Jean's hands slowly slid along Andre's wrist, he cried out in anguish, "Andre! I know that I am not going to make it. Promise me you will treat the girls right."

I promise, Jean." answered Andre.

Jean's hands slipped down past Andre's hands and with his fingers, he tried to hold on those of Andre but in seconds, Jean was sliding slowly and irretrievably down the muddy slope. In less than a minute, Jean slid screaming into the boiling lava and like the other two men before him, disappeared below the surface of the boiling red-hot lava.

Andre stared transfixed at what he saw, unable to move by the gory fascination of it all. Suddenly he felt a hand pull on his shoulder and a voice ring out, "We must go now, Doctor."

The men helped Andre to his feet and slowly the men began to edge themselves down the eastern slope. Andre had never experienced the loss of a friend. Although Jean was not a close friend, he was still a friend and the manner of his loss was one that made the loss even more unbearable. He realized that because of their short friendship, his loss would be a short one and that was better than losing one who was very close because of a long friendship. He knew that the loss of one who is close, always extends the sorrow beyond the grief experienced by the loss of a mere acquaintance.

Andre went to Monique's home to tell her about Jean's death when suddenly her brother Rene who was on the same street saw him. Rene yelled out, "You bastard! I am going to kill you."

Andre ran for his life and when he finally reached the safety of the Hayot mansion, Rene called out, "Andre Verlaine. If I see you hanging around my sister like some Casanova again, I will hunt you down and kill you."

Rachelle's parents were standing at the entrance to the mansion when Rene screamed out his threat to Andre.

Rachel's mother said in a firm voice to her husband. "I want that man out of here by tomorrow, do you understand?"

"Yes, my dear. He will be gone by tomorrow morning."

Chapter Eleven

Around seven in the morning, Monique left her house to go down to the waterfront to meet Julie Gabou, her closest friend, who was planning to organize a strike against Guerin Refinery. The sun had been up before her and its heat was becoming more apparent as the morning drew on. The volcano was quiet and the sky was clear.

Along the waterfront, a large crowd of women was assembled. These women, descended from slave stock out of Africa, had their ethnological characteristics blurred in two hundred years with all the cross breeding that had taken place. Now they were a race apart, light skinned, firmly built with supple limbs and graceful in the manner of their movements.

These women, who were referred to as *les porteuses* were the coal women of the General Atlantic Company. All day long these semi-naked figures with sweat running into their eyes, would normally empty the warehouses of Fernand Clerc, load the barrels of rum and sugar on flat bottomed tenders and ferry them out to the boats moored in the harbour. For four dollars per month, twelve hours per day, six days per week, these girls and women could carry as much as 68 kilograms in baskets on their heads at one time.

Monique knew that the women were supposed to work today since it was Monday but for reasons unknown to her, they weren't going to work at all but rather they were going to strike against the refinery.

When she arrived at the waterfront, she saw Julie surrounded by 400 coal women.

Julie yelled to her followers. "We have never called a strike on this island in its entire history but the time has come to strike!"

"Why are we striking?" asked one of the women with a little fear in her voice. She knew that Julie was the acclaimed queen of the coal women even though she was only 20 years of age, and didn't wish to incur Julie's wrath.

Julie looked down at her inquisitor and replied. "How many times in the past have we told Guerin that no one is to work on any Sundays?"

No one answered.

"Time and time again." Julie answered her own question then continued. "And because we insisted that no one was to work Sundays, the refinery has never operated on the Sabbath. Well for some reason for which Guerin won't discuss with anyone, he ordered all his employees to report to work yesterday. When we told him that it was the Sabbath, he said business comes before the Sabbath. Then he told us that anyone who didn't report to work would be summarily dismissed. Am I right?"

"Its evil to work on the Sabbath!" cried out one of the women.

"Yes and we have paid dearly for it. "Julie roared. Then she continued softly. "As most of you know, my husband Robert was crushed along with the other nineteen workers in Guerin's sugar cane field yesterday when the earth opened up and swallowed them."

"Let's march to the refinery and tell the workers to join us in refusing to work." yelled one of the women.'

"That's the spirit." replied Julie. "Who will follow me to the refinery?"

"We all will." shouted one of the women as they began to shuffle away from the barrel in which Julie stood. Soon Julie recognized Monique and jumped down off the barrel to meet her.

"Monique, it's good of you to come with us. I am hoping you can use your influence with Senator Knight should Guerin decide to have us arrested for trespassing on his property."

"I am with you on this strike, Julie. You and Robert were always close friends and anything you do is justifiable with me."

"Oh, oh!" exclaimed Julie, here comes the foreman."

A man approached the women walking off the job and demanded that they return to work.

"Don't talk to him. Just keep walking." shouted Julie.

The foreman approached Julie and yelled to her, "You may be the high queen around here but this will be your last day on the job if you and these women don't return to your work!"

"You can't fire us all." laughed one of the women.

"No, but I can fire her and you and a few others as an example." retorted the foreman.

The women ignored him and continued to march away until all of them were on the road leading to the Guerin Refinery a few kilometres away.

An hour later, they approached the refinery, and as previously planned; all the women entered the refinery and began to talk to the men and women working there. In less than ten minutes the entire plant had shut down and all the workers were chatting with the coal women.

Suddenly there was a commotion at one end of the refinery, and Julie and Monique went over to see what it was about.

A man's angry voice rung out, "You will all return to work or I will fire every one of you."

"Fire us and you will have to shut down the refinery." jeered another in response. The rest of the workers began laughing at the man in the white suit who had threatened them with mass firings.

"Where is your leader?" asked the man in the white.

"I am their leader." replied Julie.

"You!" exclaimed the man in startled surprise.

"What surprises you, the fact that I am a mulatto or that I am a woman?"

"I am Doctor Guerin," the man in white said.

"Then you are the man we wish to speak to," replied Julie. Then she continued. "Why did you order all your employees to work on the Sabbath?"

"That's my business," retorted Guerin.

"No damn you!" screamed Julie. "It's our business."

"If I choose to have my employees work on a Sunday, then it's my decision to make."

"No, it's the decision of the employees to make."

Guerin smiled then said. "Then they made it, didn't they because they came."

A voice rang out from the back of the crowd, "We came because you let it be known that you would fire anyone who didn't"

"That's true." added another. "What kind of decision is that?"

Guerin stammered. "Everyone who worked yesterday will be paid for their labour."

"Will you pay for the labour of the twenty workers in the field who were killed when the earth opened up and crushed them?" screamed Julie.

"That was a most unfortunate accident." Guerin replied softly.

"It was God's vengeance on those who worked on the Sabbath." another called out.

"What is it you want of me?" asked Guerin.

"We want to have the rest of this day off to use as we see fit." replied Julie.

"Yea!" yelled the crowd.

"Impossible!" Guerin said.

"Then we will take the day off anyhow."

"Just a minute," said Guerin. "Have several of your representatives meet with me at my office on the hill and we will see if we can reach a satisfactory agreement."

The crowd looked at Julie in silence then she answered. "Very well, Doctor Guerin." Then turning to Monique and a friend of her husband who worked at the refinery, she asked "Would you two join me to discuss this situation with Doctor Guerin?"

Both nodded in the affirmative.

"Fine." said Guerin. "The rest of you continue working."

The crowd looked at Julie, and then she nodded and said "OK, we will report to you as to what is decided. The coal women can return to the city and wait for me."

Dr. Guerin, Julie, Monique and Pierre, the former friend of Julie's husband, walked out of the refinery to Guerin's office which was in his house on the hill overlooking the refinery.

When they had all seated and Guerin had ordered tea, he started the conversation. "I hope that you are aware of my deep sorrow for the loss of those unfortunates struck down in the cane field."

"God acts in a mysterious way." Julie said with her head bowed.

"I don't think God would strike down those innocent people because I ordered them to work on the Sabbath."

"You are speaking blasphemy in the sight of God." said Monique.

"I don't want to appear sacrilegious but surely you are not blaming God for the death of those twenty workers?"

"I am blaming you, Doctor Guerin." replied Julie.

From the direction of the refinery came the familiar sounds of the sugar factory coming back to life; the rustle of bundled sheaths of cane being fed to conveyor belts which carried them in a never ending stream from the wooden-wheeled carts into the factory itself, and the steady rumble of the dynamo which drove the machinery that chopped, shredded, and crushed the cane into juice.

Suddenly there was the sound of screaming coming from the kitchen. Seconds later, a woman raced through the house to the office where the others were meeting. "The ants, the ants!" she screamed, as she slapped her body trying to get them off.

The cry was taken up in other parts of the villa and from the sugar refinery. Guerin rushed outside and saw his head overseer, organizing the workers to fight the plague of ants and centipedes which had swarmed in from the banks of the Blanche River.

They had been driven farther and farther down the slopes of Pelee by the ash falls. The ants, speckled, yellowish creatures, whose bite stung like red hot needles, and the centipedes, many of them a foot long, with mouths capable of biting through shoe leather, crawled over the ground by the thousands. They swarmed into the factory, creating panic among the workers and bringing terror to the horses as the ants and centipedes climbed into their fetlocks.

Inside the house, the rattle of shutters being closed could be heard as the villa prepared to resists the invaders.

Monique stood terror-struck. She knew what these insects were capable of doing. She had heard that in 1851, when the volcano had covered the jungles with ash, the creatures had swept into coastal areas, creating havoc and death. In certain areas, they had destroyed plantations and hamlets. Babies in their beds had been eaten alive. Immense balls of living ants had rolled into the area of the north of the island, drifted down the coast, and came ashore at St. Pierre. It had taken months to rout the insects and drive them back to the higher slopes of the volcano. Behind them they had left a trail of dead domestic animals and humans.

Soon the centipedes and ants began to swarm over the wall of the villa. Then they began to crawl through the cracks in the shutters. They swarmed in all directions, and soon everyone in the villa was tearing at their clothes to pull the insects off, slapping their legs and jumping up and down to avoid the biting insects crawling up their legs.

Already, the centipedes had moved upstairs, lurking in the bedclothes and in the closets. Monique and Julie had gone up the stairs in hopes of avoiding them but instead were followed by them. They swung brooms at the centipedes and the ants to squash them. The insects crawled up the handles and Julie felt the prickling of feet on the back of her dress. A centipede had crawled up her dress and was ready to bite her neck. She screamed and backed into the wall in hopes of crushing the insect. She could hear the crackling of the insect's body as she pressed against the wall but when she stepped from the wall, she carried with her the ants that had been climbing the wall and had now attached themselves to her dress.

Outside, the battle was in full progress. Barrels of oil, used for lubricating the machinery, had been emptied into the yard. Thousands of ants filed into the thick morass and were trapped, then the oil was set afire and the ants began crackling in the heat.

A bucket brigade, led by Eugene Guerin, the eldest son of Dr. Guerin, was pouring buckets over the terrified horses to drown the insects. Another group of men and women were systematically beating their way through the sugar factory, crushing the insects under sacks soaked in oil.

Inside the villa, centipede after centipede fell under the flailing pans and flat irons of the household. Retreating under attack, both the centipedes and the ants displayed cunning, fighting to the last bite. The centipedes, each a foot long, with pink bellies and violet heads were darting from room to room with stunning speed, their legs moving in panic causing their bodies to lengthen and shorten.

Some of the maids poured iron cauldrons of boiling water over the creatures. There was a crackling sound as the steaming water poured over the centipedes. Some curled up like a protective cocoon while others continued the attack. The centipedes on a fontal attack were an unnerving sight.

An hour later, the men and women continued to stamp on them, beat them with brooms and sticks until the remaining insects had moved back to the banks of the river. There the ants rolled themselves into balls and floated down the river and out to sea. The centipedes for the most part seemed able to float on the surface and they too were washed out to sea.

Dr Guerin, Monique, Julie and Pierre sat down again to discuss the pending strike, each one looking out for ants and centipedes still prowling about.

Guerin started the conversation again from where the negotiators had left off. "You wanted to know why I insisted that all my employees work Sunday. Very well, I will tell you. Saturday evening I had heard that a number of the captains of the cargo boats in the harbour were threatening to sail with their holds unfilled because of the way the volcano was acting up. If they sailed before unloading the cargo, that means I would have to wait another month before the next batch of cargo boats come to the island. Now unless the volcano abates, it will ruin my crop. There is still a greater possibility that the ash from the volcano, if it increases, will clog up the machinery of the processing plant.

Julie turned to the others and said. "Well then it would seem that the only matter for discussion is what payment should be given for the extra day's work." The others nodded in agreement.

Andre had realized that he had to leave the Hayot house so just as the sun came over the hill behind the house, he left with his belongings and started walking down the road towards the city. There, he would stay at the main hotel, or perhaps Monique would put him up or perhaps he might spend his remaining days on the island's capital, Fort du France.

As he approached the city, he saw a long column of people marching north towards the Blanche River and thought, perhaps the villagers of Prechure were returning to their homes despite the warnings.

He arrived in the city and headed towards the public gardens. After several hours, he decided to call on Monique, knowing that she would be up by nine in the morning. He knocked on her door not knowing for sure as to whether she would be opening it. There was no response to his knocking on her door. He presumed that Monique wasn't home, so he began to wander around the streets of the mulatto quarter looking for her.

Somewhere in the distance, he could hear voices but he wasn't sure as to whether they were screaming or just shouting. He followed the sound of the voices and suddenly as he came to an intersection, he saw hundreds of people running towards him. They ran past him and when he pulled one towards him, the man wriggled free crying, "They're coming!"

Andre decided what ever it was that was coming, he wanted no part of it and followed the frightened townspeople to wherever they were going. The crowd ran down several more streets with Andre trailing and then they stopped for a moment, and then turned towards the direction they came. Andre let them pass because as now he was determined to see for himself what was causing the panic.

As he stood alone on the street, he saw a couple of yellowish-brown snake-like things slithering towards him. At once he recognized them as fer-de-lance snakes, one of the most deadliest of all vipers.

Two metres or more in length, the fer-de-lance attacks with bewildering speed. Within the span of a few heartbeats, the pierced flesh of its victim chills and becomes soft and swollen. Spots appear on the skin, and death comes with an icy coldness creeping through the bloodstream. Later there is a terrifying necrosis of the tissues, the flesh appearing to hang from the bone, and the colours of its putrefaction resembling the hues of vegetable decay: ghastly grays, pinks and yellows that cover the victim's skin.

His eyes were fixed on the slithering reptiles and just as one of them was about to attack him, he come out of his hypnotized state and turned and ran up the street.

Fanning out, hundreds of the snakes slithered deep into the mulato quarter, attacking anyone in sight, writhing, stretching, springing, striking; all in one blinding movement. The reptiles driven down the mountain in search of food because of the same ash which drove the insects to the sea were converging on the mulatto quarter from every direction.

The flight from the mulato quarter would have been a full scale stampede had it not been for the troops summoned by Mayor Fouche. Pushing their way through the screaming mob, the soldiers advanced on the houses, shooting the snakes on sight.

The townspeople now quieted down and calmed by the musket fire, stopped to watch the battle. Soon the muskets were aided by another weapon; huge stray cats that lived on the streets of St. Pierre. Attracted by the excitement, the cats had descended upon the mulato quarter. The cats, whether through hunger or bravery, advanced on the serpents. The cats would feint, tease and try to draw the serpents to strike first. And when they struck, their claws mangled the heads of the snakes. Again the snakes would strike, and again the cats would sweep the heads aside, inflicting further damage. Blinded, skin deeply torn, eye sockets hanging loose, the snakes were stunned. Then, the cats would leap on them, bashing their heads to the ground, while keen white teeth severed the vertebrae of the fer-de-lances.

In an hour, over one hundred snakes had been either shot, clubbed or bitten to death. By then, fifty people and five times that number of animals had been bitten by the vipers and had died hideously from their venom.

The Blance River with the Guerin Sugar Refinery at its base, begins its journey to the sea from somewhere near the summit of Mt. Pelee. The river derives its source from inside the mountain and pours out of the crevices of large rock formations. It cascades down the mountain, through the green jungle then through a clearing where the sugarcane fields are situated, then past the refinery and out to sea.

Shortly after twelve noon, about a thousand metres up Mt. Pelee and several hundred metres up from the jungle, the ground began to shake uncontrollably. Suddenly a giant wall of mud rose into the air; nearly ten metres in height, hung for a brief moment, then flopped down on the jungle below it and began to descend down the mountain with ever increasing speed towards the coastline.

As the brown steaming mass hurtled towards the sea, it gathered up trees and huge boulders and carried them, increasing the weight of the monster wave fast approaching the coastline. It cut a swath through the jungle and by the time it had reached the clearing at the edge of the jungle, it was over sixty metres across and just over a thirty metres high; a wall of millions of tonnes of mud, lava, boiling gases, boulders and jungle debris traveling at a speed of over a hundred and twenty kilometres an hour.

In the Guerin villa, the occupants could feel the ground shaking and could hear a roaring and hissing sounds coming from the direction of the volcano.

"We had better see what's going on outside." said Guerin "The mountain may be acting up again

Chapter Twelve

Everyone in the villa got up and went outside. Monique noticed that a few of the persons who were outside the factory were staring at the volcano. She turned the direction of her gaze towards it and was momentarily dumbfounded at what she saw.

The wall of mud was now thirty metres high and a quarter of a kilometre across. It was halfway down the sugar cane fields. She couldn't see anything behind it.

She turned to Julie but Julie wasn't beside her. She was running towards the factory. As Julie neared the entrance, she called out to those inside, "Hurry! Hurry! Get out or you will be lost! A mud slide is coming down the mountain!"

Monique turned and ran towards the road leading away from the factory with many of the workers following close behind her. The mountainous wall rolled over the villa, and approached the factory. Julie and the others exited from the factory door and began to run away from the mountainous death fast approaching them.

Within seconds, the wall of mud hung over the factory like a huge wave for a split second, and then crashed down upon the building. The entire factory was engulfed with mud with the exception of the tip of the 24-metre smoke stack. The wall of mud, although slowing down under the impact of having struck the Guerin Refinery, was rolling onwards towards the sea, spreading even wider as it moved. The slide of earth, rocks, trees and debris hit the sea with a terrifying impact, causing the sea to rise and back away from the land not unlike the undertow rushing out to meet a wave.

A few moments later, a boiling stream of water burst forth from the mountain, leaping all obstacles in gigantic bounds, flowing down over the mud and onto where the refinery had been. Twenty-five workers, who survived the impact of the slide but were trapped in the mud, were then scalded to death by the boiling water.

Following the boiling water, came a torrent of water-laden rush of boulders and earth pouring down the side of the mountain. The lake that was part way up the mountain had burst its banks and was cascading down to the coast, leveling the mud as it flowed over it until it rushed over the entire area where the mud had been. The region was razed and a mud plain was formed from the edge of the jungle to the sea. The few survivors wept as they stared at what had been a factory but was now only a smokestack, marking the grave of well over a hundred victims.

Andre had heard that Monique had been seen down at the waterfront so he went to the wharf of the Trans Atlantic Company. Perhaps, he thought, Julie Gaban would know where Monique was. He was unaware of Julie's untimely death. On his way to the wharf, he noticed that Mt. Pelee was emitting thick gray smoke. It hung in the still air and then it began to drift down on the countryside. Slowly the smoke blanketed the city and then headed out to sea. The sun was blotted out and the sky darkened.

Andre worked his way down the waterfront and arrived at the wharf a few minutes later. He saw a man on the wharf and asked him why it was deserted. He replied that the women had gone to the Guerin Refinery to hold a strike.

Andre turned to leave but his eyes were drawn out to sea. Perhaps it was the sudden gush of wind, blowing the smoke back over the city and into the hinterland that caused him to face the sea, but now he couldn't take his eyes off the horizon.

At first, he thought it was a trick of light northward but it appeared to him as if the horizon along the coast had disappeared and the normally even line between the sea and sky was moving. He looked out in the harbour and saw a number of the boats weighing anchor preparing for sea. He noticed with curiosity that the water was rising and dropping amongst the piers like immense swells.

Again he looked up the coast to the horizon and he observed that the horizon was becoming more agitated than before. He noticed a small wave slapping against the waterfront. It was followed by another one, slightly larger than the first. Then another leaped against the timbers of the wharfs. It was then that he noticed a change in the waves. The third wave and fourth waves had distinct runoffs, sweeping well back into the harbour. Suddenly in the distance, he saw a huge wall of water rushing towards the harbour. Nearly twenty metres high, and sounding like a million hissing snakes, it headed towards St. Pierre. As the wall of water weighing billions of tonnes moved quickly towards the city, Andre realized that the wave was going to roll over the waterfront.

The top of the wave began curling and the spindrift flew high in the air. At the base of the wave he could see the harbour's flotsam being drawn up to the top of the wave, only to be dropped as the uppermost part of the wave crashed into the sea. The roar of the crashing wave was deafening. He knew that to remain on the waterfront would mean instant death.

Turning, he fled into the town, shouting out warnings. "Monster wave! Monster wave!"

Ahead of the wave rolled rocks that had been earlier blasted out of the mountain and had rolled down its slopes on the crests of the mudflow. Now they were being rolled along the ocean floor by the enormous wave heading towards the city.

Andre glanced backwards and watched with terror as the wave hit two of the Italian sailing boats moored in the habour. Their moorings were uprooted, and the boats were lifted high up the churning wall of water and borne on its crest towards the waterfront.

As Andre continued to run up the street shouting warnings, other townspeople began realizing what was coming from the sea and joined him on his race from the waterfront. Soon hundreds of people, screaming and tearing at each other to get up the street, began to clog the escape routes. Within seconds, a human flood poured up from the depths of the waterfront. Doors and shutters were closed and then the inhabitants began running away from the wave to take refuge on the heights.

In the streets, the panic increased as the crowd grew greater. Cowards when frightened, can be cruel in their zeal to escape their fate. They will abandon their loved ones just as easily as they abandon the stranger on the street. Men fleeing from the waterfront trampled over women and children.

Andre passed the English Colonial Bank just as three of the clerks began to barricade the door against the torrent about to pour into the city. Overhead, the dust clouds thinned as a warm breeze blew in from the sea, sweeping the ash back over the hinterland. Mt. Pelee growled as if to join in the foray.

Again Andre turned to look at the monster from the sea fast approaching him. He was only three blocks from the edge of the waterfront. The fourth street would take him past the main street which was perpendicular to the one he was on but fortunately it rose up a steep hill.

He looked back again. He couldn't believe what he saw. The two sailing boats were higher than the buildings on the waterfront. For a second they hung there in a critical imbalance, then in a powerful surge, the steep gray wall of water which supported them, crashed into the first row of buildings. The boats passed right over the first row of buildings and were dumped with shattering crunches in the street behind the buildings. The great mass of frothing water moved forward and a line of warehouses were ripped from their foundations and then stood on end as if glued to the wall of water.

Andre ran even harder, his lungs bursting as he started the tiring climb up the steep street. Behind him he could hear the splintering of timber, and the smashing of buildings, but above all, the roar of the monster wave as it moved closer to him. The wave swept the debris against other buildings like battering rams. The second row of buildings succumbed to the weight and force of the wave and the debris it carried with it.

Again he looked behind him and couldn't see the first and second streets on the waterfront as they were completely submerged beneath the sea. Carts, barrels, dead animals, human bodies, boats and even whole buildings were swept up like bathtub toys, stacked, smashed, and submerged in the flooded streets. The wave roared into

Rue Victor Hugo, its murky water reaching upwards to the upper balconies. Andre knew he wouldn't get up the hill in time to save himself but thought he might be able to get onto the top floor of one of the buildings next to him. He knew that as the wave continued up the street, its force would be spent and although the wave would rise up inside the building, it might not smash it.

The wave was only several hundred metres behind him so he dashed into the doorway and began to run up the stairs. He had just turned in the stairwell when he heard the water smash into the doorway and windows on the first floor. It got dark suddenly as the daylight from the main floor was blotted out from the wave smashing through the windows. He heard the gurgling water as it rose up the stairs behind him and in seconds he reached the second floor. There were no other stairs to climb so he ran into a room facing the waterfront. The wave smashed through the second floor windows and Andre felt absolute terror as the onrushing water smashed him against the wall on the other side of the room. He struggled against the water as it tried to engulf him in its embrace.

He felt the wave tossing him about the room like a rag doll and just as he was losing consciousness, the water began to draw him toward the doorway. It sucked him down the stairs like a piece of wood being sucked into a sewer. He saw the water receding out of the doorway to the street but he managed to grab a hold of a railing before the receding water would suck him outside.

He stood at the doorway, mesmerized as the runoff began its journey back to the sea. The water, try as it might, could not resist the gravitational pull that was being exerted on it to take it back from where it came. It started its retreat to the sea with a great sighing and hissing, taking as much debris and struggling humans as it could pry from the houses and the streets.

When it had returned to the sea, just minutes after smashing into the city, the downtown sector looked like a city of splinters. Whole sections of the waterfront including the large warehouses were smashed like kindling. The sailing boats, lifted originally by the receding water, now lay on their sides, their masts stripped of their sails, their decks splintered, and their crew dead or dying.

As Andre headed back to the waterfront, he heard the volcano roaring again and looked behind him and saw huge billowing columns of black smoke being shot out of the crater of the volcano and high into the sky. Then the column of smoke and ash began to spread out across the sky. Minutes later, the sun was blotted out again and as the ash began to fall on the city, darkness came upon the inhabitants not unlike when there is an eclipse of the sun.

Choking and blindly stumbling over bodies and debris, Andre, while groping towards the waterfront, overheard a few voices talking about the orphanage having been swept away. His heart began to beat wildly. He headed along Victor Hugo and then down a side street where the orphanage was situated. He feared the worst as he approached the location of the orphanage. It was difficult to see where he was going because of the darkness that shrouded the city but he could occasionally see the outlines of the broken buildings because of the flashes of lightening that lit up the area. Then rain began to fall on the city. The rain kept the ash down and gradually the sun began to filter its way through the smoke from the volcano to the crowds of people, milling about aimlessly, looking for the bodies of their loved ones.

When Andre reached the site of the severely damaged orphanage, a woman approached him and cried, "Oh Doctor Verlain!" Andre recognized the woman as being one of the matrons working in the orphanage.

"It was horrible!" she wept. "No one survived! The wave just smashed into the building and took everyone away!"

"What happened to Rachelle Hayot? Did you see her?" asked Andre as he grabbed the woman's shaking arm.

"She's not here." sobbed the woman.

"What happened to her?" pleaded Andre.

"She wasn't here." replied the sobbing woman.

"You mean she didn't report to work this morning?"

"I didn't see her at all today."

Andre breathed a sign of relief as he realized that Rachelle was probably too upset from the previous night, to report to work and therefore was still safe at her father's plantation. He left the crying woman and decided to go to the Guerin sugar refinery to locate Monique. On the way to the refinery he passed a number of survivors of the mud avalanche.

"Have any of you seen Monique Rousseau at the Refinery?"

The survivors looked at him and nodded and replied "No,"

"Surely you could tell me if Julie Gabou was there?"

"They're all dead." one of the men said quietly.

Andre's heart began to beat wildly again and he blurted out, "What happened? Was it the wave?"

One of the men looked at him and in a quizzical manner asked, "What wave?"

"The one that came from the sea."

"It was no wave from the sea that hit the refinery."

"What happened to the refinery?" asked Andre as he grabbed the man's shoulder.

The man pulled himself away instead of answering and began to run after the others heading towards the city.

Andre continued on to the refinery and in half an hour, he came upon a plain of mud. In the middle of it, he could see the black smoke stack of the refinery just sticking out of the mud. He looked up towards the mountain and could see the mud plain extending up past the cane fields and the forest. He sat down and cried realizing that Monique must have been buried somewhere under the plain, never to be found again.

Andre headed back to the city and by mid afternoon was walking amidst the dead and dying in the city. Along the lower half of Victor Hugo, the devastation was almost total. Shops on both sides of the street had been crushed under the wall of water.

Furniture, clothing and bodies were scattered everywhere. The washer women who used to wash the clothes on the banks of the Roxelane River had been swept away by the huge wave as it rushed up the river.

In the mulato quarter, the searchers recovered sixty-eight bodies of the home owners who had been drowned in their tin-roofed houses. The wave had uprooted the trees and killed the goats, cows, and small Creole horses at their tether posts. Many of the townspeople in the mulato quarter began to evacuate their homes, many of which were a complete shambles. They piled their few belongings, mattresses and small furniture high in their hand carts. In the confusion of the haste and panic, they pushed and dragged their carts to the upper reaches of the city.

With the boulders washed ashore, came some of the bodies which had been washed out to sea from the Roxlane River the previous days.

The concourse of men, women and children weeping, crying out for mercy from what they thought might come next, trekked toward the hill overlooking the city. Andre was part of that concourse.

"Andre!" a voice cried out.

Andre turned and was facing Mr. Hurard, the newspaper editor. He was a big man who wore glasses although now he was without them as they got lost in the disaster.

"Andre, I wonder if I could impose on you to come with me to a meeting?"

"Yes, of course."

The two men walked through the debris of the mulato quarter and then up Rue Victor Hugo to the city hall. They pushed their way through the crowd blocking the doorway to the building. Then they were escorted by soldiers to the mayor's office.

"Gentlemen." the mayor called out. "This meeting will come to order." I have asked Mr. Hurard to invite Doctor Verlaine to attend this meeting. I trust no one has any objections."

Marcel Hayot smiled at Andre and said. "The doctor is always welcome to such meetings."

Chapter Thirteen

"Gentlemen," continued the mayor. "As you know, Governor Mouttet has asked us to write him a report on the current state of the volcano and as such we are the Governor's Commission of Inquiry. Now I wish to have this report written this afternoon so that I can take it to the Governor's residence by late afternoon. We will first hear from Professor Landes."

"Thank you, Your Honour," replied the bearded professor. "I have carefully studied the situation with some of my fellow commissioners and we have come to the opinion that despite the recent happenings, the city of St. Pierre is in no immediate danger from the volcano. What does disturb me is that we have lost a great deal of the plant life in our beloved gardens in the Jardin des Plantes."

Marcel interjected angrily. "You speak of your plants being ruined and yet you say nothing of the Guerin Refinery and the loss of all those lives there and of the huge wave that just wiped out our waterfront and killed hundreds in the streets. What kind of man are you?"

"Oh, I am aware of the unfortunate loss of life and the destruction of property but I have only written six pages about the ruin of the garden which I must insist be included in the report." The professor shuffled the pages and handed them to the mayor.

"Very well, professor, we will include them," said the mayor indifferently as he reached for the sheets of paper. "And now perhaps we will hear from the Garrison Commander."

The Commander of the garrison was a beefy man but despite his strength, he spoke in a worried tone of voice. "The people are getting out of hand, your Worship. There is widespread panic in the city."

"To what would you attribute that?" asked the mayor of St. Pierre.

The Commander's face turned crimson. "To what, you ask?" asked the garrison commander in a near screaming voice. "You know about the mountain, the waterfront, the refinery, the smashed buildings and missing bridges, not to mention the hundreds dead and you still have the audacity to ask me such a fool question?"

"Well," said the mayor, "We are not ignoring these happenings, but perhaps we have seen the last of them."

"I doubt it." said Father Roche.

"Why do you say that?" asked the mayor.

"Well Sir, when I studied volcanology, I remembered a few of the important things to look for."

"Such as what?" asked professor Landes.

"The intensity and the frequency of the eruptions and the colour of the smoke, that's what."

"The colour of the smoke?" asked the professor with a sneer.

"Yes," replied the priest. "The colour tells us much. When it's white, most of the smoke is really steam, condensation from the heat. When it's yellow, most of the smoke is mud, and when the smoke is black, it's because of small pieces of lava shooting out of the volcano."

Fernand Clerc interjected. "I think we had better also mention in the report that the telephone cable is broken and because of that, we don't have a link with the other islands."

"Fortunately, we still have contact with Paris through the transatlantic Cable." said the mayor.

"Perhaps I might suggest—," began Andre.

"Yes, of course Doctor." the mayor responded.

"Well gentlemen, it seems that the Roxlane River is overflowing its banks and there is only one bridge and if it goes, we'll loose contact with the other half of the city."

"A good point," said Marcel. "I understand that the British Consul, Mister James Japp, is stranded on the island in the river in which the residence is situated."

"Yes, that's true but he has communicated with us by a heliograph to advise us that they have enough food and water for another week." said the Commander.

"We will make a report on the river, Doctor Verlaine" said the Mayor. "Thank you for bringing it to our attention."

"What about the Blanche River." asked Roche.

"I was there not too long ago," replied Mr. Hurard. "There is no river left. Just a valley of mud."

"Well, the bridge was washed out anyhow so perhaps when the mud hardens, we can walk across where the river used to be." said Father Roche.

"No need to mention the Blanche River in the report." said Mayor Fouche.

"Does anyone have anything to add?"

"Yes, I do." replied Colonel Gerbault. I think typhus has broken out in the mulatto quarter."

"Typhus?" the others in the room exclaimed in unison.

"What makes you think it's typhus?" asked Andre

"There have been quite a few persons reporting to the hospital claiming that they are suffering from dizziness, headaches, muscle pains, chills and continuous vomiting."

"Has this been more noticeable with the negro population than the others?"

"Yes" replied the colonel. "Why do you ask?"

"Because" continued Andre "What you are describing is Smallpox?"

"Smallpox!" exclaimed the others in the room.

"Yes." said Andre

"How can we be sure that it's the Pox?" asked Mayor Fouche.

"Usually a rash appears on the fourth day." said Andre. "The skin on the head and limbs become sprinkled with spots which fill with a fluid, first clear, then later becoming a pus-like substance, resembling a boil. Then they open and drain, then are scabbed over. Then these boil-like substances heal in about three weeks. Of course the scars remain. I have seen these symptoms in the mulatto quarter."

"If the pox doesn't kill the victim first." retorted Professor Landes. "If Smallpox has struck Martinique you can be sure it is probably the mild form called alastrim, a type that is common in the West Indies especially amongst the negro population. The fatality rate here would be about two percent."

"What can we do?" asked Mayor Fouche.

"Have you any vaccine?"

"Not enough." replied Colonel Gerbault, who had earlier been placed in charge of medical stores.

"Then I suggest that we check every house in the mulatto quarter and if anyone has it, burn their house down."

"Do you know what you are asking?" asked Professor Landes."

"Not asking," replied Andre, "Ordering!" If you don't want this island infested, you must fight the disease with everything we have. With this wave smashing the city, you will find that the disease will spread because of the unburied bodies laying about."

"I refuse to order the burning of houses in this city," retorted Mayor Fouche.

"Would you rather see your city decimated by the pox?" asked Andre.

"You don't understand Doctor." continued the mayor. "If you burn the houses, and the fire gets out of control, we might end up losing the entire city."

"But—" Andre began.

"My answer is final Doctor. There will be no burning of homes on St. Pierre. We must find a more suitable way to combat the pox."

Professor Landes leaned towards Andre and whispered "We will have to bury the bodies in common graves and cover them with quicklime."

"I will help with the vaccination if you like," said Andre in return. He didn't want to handle pox-infested bodies.

"Very well Gentlemen, if there is nothing further to discuss, I will write up this report and take it to the Governor by the late afternoon," said Mayor Fouche.

As the men began to leave the Mayor's office, Marcel took Andre aside and said, "Andre, I am sorry that things hadn't worked out for you and Rachelle as you would like. It seems ironic that you came to this island to marry the girl and end up fighting small pox with the rest of us."

"And the rest of the elements that seem to be hitting the island." said Andre.

"Yes," replied Marcel, "This week has been one that no islander has ever seen before." Then he added. "I see from the dampness of your clothing, that you must have been hit by the wave."

"Yes sir." said Andre. "I am glad that Rachelle didn't go to the orphanage today."

"Thank you, my boy. It was fate that saved her life today. If she hadn't quarreled with you last night and been upset this morning because of it, she would have gone to the orphanage and drowned like the others." Then he continued, "Are you going to marry the other girl?"

Andre wondered how Marcel knew about White Flower when he replied, "No sir."

"I am glad, my boy." said Marcel. "Mixed marriages never really work—at least not in France."

"She was killed at the Guerin Refinery." said Andre in response.

Marcel took a long look at Andre then said sadly, "I sincerely hope you will forgive me Andre for my ill-timed remark."

"Yes, of course I will." replied Andre. "And now Sir, I must go to the hospital to pick up the vaccine."

"Good luck, Andre." said Marcel as he shook Andre's hand.

"Same to you, Sir."

Both left, each his own way.

Andre hurried over to the hospital, and after being given vaccine and hypodermic needles, he joined some of the other staff heading towards the mulatto quarter. There, he saw many of the townspeople lined up for the shot in the arm they believed would save them from the pox.

Hours later, as the sun was setting, he saw large cauldrons of tar set afire every hundreds of metres or so.

"What is that for?" he asked a doctor working next to him. "That is an ancient ritual that most of the inhabitants indulge in when a disease strikes any of the islands. It's supposed to purify the air."

"I hardly think that it would purify the air." replied Andre.

"No, but it sure lets the incoming boats know that there is a plague in St. Pierre and to stay away."

"Oh no!" blurted out Andre.

"What's the matter?"

"The *Rormania* is supposed to return to France with me on it. If they see the tar barrels burning then they won't allow me on board."

"When is it due?"

" The Seventh."

"Well, perhaps we will have the pox under control by then."

Suddenly Andre saw Senator Knight near the houses. He excused himself and walked to the Senator.

"Senator!" yelled Andre.

The Senator turned and smiled as Andre approached him. "I am glad that you have survived the day, Doctor Verlaine."

"Thank you, Sir." replied Andre. "I am sorry that Monique wasn't lucky."

"What do you mean?"

"She was lost at the Guerin Refinery."

"Who told you that, Doctor?"

"Several people told me that she had gone to the refinery with Julie Gabour to deal with some sort of strike. There was a landslide and she along with others were buried under tons of hot mud."

"Doctor," continued Senator Knight, "I was talking to her less than half an hour ago."

"You were?" Andre choked, "Where? Where?"

"Up on the hill." said the senator as he pointed to the hill back of St. Pierre. "She is there with many of the townspeople."

Andre turned and ran up the street, then briefly turned to yell, "Thanks! Many thanks."

Andre stumbled over timbers, bodies and fallen trees as he ran up the hill overlooking the city. Fifteen minutes later, he was on the pathway at the crest of the hill realizing that it would only be by luck that he would find Monique. It appeared to him that the entire population of St. Pierre was camped on the hill. He looked on both sides of the paths criss-crossing the hill and moved in closer to the small fires which townspeople huddled around to keep warm. Some fires had entire families huddled around them, some, only a few persons.

At every fire, he kept asking, "Has anyone seen Monique Rousseau?" or "Has anyone seen White Flower?"

For hours, he tramped all over the hill, asking, prodding at the forms sleeping in the grass, and always the same result. "No, never heard of her." or "Is she white or mulatto?" and "Who?"

He found a quiet spot near the bluff overlooking the city and watched as the lights in the city flicked like little fireflies. In the distance, he could hear the voices of the mulattos singing, and he began to feel very drowsy. As the singing continued, his eyes began to get very tired.

"Andre." a woman's voice called out gently from behind him. "Andre, I have been looking for you."

Andre could faintly hear the voice and realized it was a voice that was familiar to him. He slowly turned and stared at the woman's face.

"Monique! Monique, you're here!" he stammered. "I have searched for you all night."

"I looked for you also, Andre," replied Monique as she embraced him. "I heard that you were in the city but I thought you had drowned in the wave."

"I nearly did, but managed to get away from its fury." replied Andre. "How did you survive the avalanche?"

"I ran up the hill overlooking Doctor Guerin's villa just as the mud came down the mountain."

"We have been spared for some reason, Monique, but I don't know why."

"Did Rachelle escape the wave?"

"Yes. As a matter of fact, she was nowhere near it. She didn't report to the orphanage today."

"Have you seen her at all today, Andre?"

No. She and I have broken up for good."

I am sorry to hear that, Andre. You have come a long way just to return alone."

I don't think so, Monique." replied Andre. "I came to Martinique to marry Rachelle, but instead, I fell in love with you."

Andre, you shouldn't say that."

Why not? It's true, you know."

Andre," Monique said softly, "I realize that in these few short days, we have become very fond of each other but when Thursday comes, you will leave for France without me, because destiny has ruled it so. It is not in the cards that you should return to Paris with a mulato girl."

Destiny is what we make for ourselves, Monique. It is not just some fate over which we have no control."

I believe in a Superior Being that rules our lives," said Monique. "and He decides that I shall not go to France with you."

Do you love me, Monique?" asked Andre as he grasped her hand. She replied that she did. Andre responded, "Then believe me when I say that I shall return to France with you as my bride."

What would your friends say in Paris when they realize that your wife is coloured?"

You are not coloured."

"But Andre." continued Monique. "My mother was a mulato and her blood runs through my veins."

Andre moved closer to Monique and whispered in her ear, "I'm not in love with your mother. I'm in love with you. I don't care if you have black ink running through your veins. If my friends can't accept you, that is their loss, not mine. Let me assure you Monique, that in the last analysis, love is the real reflection of the worth of a man and woman for without it, there can be no reflection of them at all."

Monique had at last found a man with compassion.

Chapter Fourteen

As the two of them walked along the winding path leading down the hill, Monique spoke again. "Andre, as the years go on, you may not feel that our love is enough. A man must have his friends."

"If I have to choose between having you or my friends, I will choose you." replied Andre as he leaned over to kiss her.

"Andre, a man should be able to have both a wife and his friends. Neither should suffer because of the other."

"Monique, I am willing to take the chance that I can have both."

"That's what it is, Andre. A chance."

"It's more than just a chance. I love you Monique, and I know that we can be happy in Paris."

"I believe you, Andre when you say that you love me and I hope you believe me when I say that I truly love you but I know that it wouldn't work out."

"Why do you say that?"

"I have seen others try it out and their marriages failed. They ended up being alone and with no friends."

"Because they failed is no reason why our marriage would fail. Remember, what you have seen of those failures in the mixed marriages is here in St. Pierre."

Monique thought for a few seconds then said "Let me think it over, Andre."

"I know that if you decide to come with me to Paris, we will be very happy." said Andre.

"Are you still staying at Hayot plantation?" Monique asked.

"No, I left this morning."

"You are welcome to stay at my place if you wish."

"Thanks Monique." said Andre. "Shall we go to your place now?"

"Yes, if you like."

Together the two of them, hand in hand, descended the hill and walked through the darkened streets towards the Mulatto quarter. There were still people moving about in the city, some of them pushing carts along the cobblestone roads with their cargo of bodies, dug out of the ruins of the city. One woman was desperately trying to stay close behind one cart as it headed towards a common grave, carrying the bodies of her husband and their two children.

In the city of Fort du France, the delegation from Mayor Fouche's office was in the residence of Governor Mouttet discussing their report.

"Excellency." said Mayor Fouche, "I am pleased to bring you the report that you have been waiting for."

The governor browsed through it and then said, "It seems to be concise. However I am wondering if St. Pierre will be subjected to any more attacks from Mt. Pelee,"

Professor Landes said, "You have my personal assurance, Excellency, that we have no further need to worry about anymore trouble from the mountain."

"I respect your opinion, Professor, but I don't think I can accept your personal assurance that the mountain will not erupt anymore. Now if you are an emissary of God, I will hang on your every word."

"What I meant, Sir, is that it doesn't appear to be getting any worse."

"Not getting any worse, you say!" retorted Father Roche. "How can you say that when you know that a mud slide wiped out the Guerin Refinery and that a huge wave wiped out the waterfront of St. Pierre?"

"What's all this?" asked the Governor turning to Mayor Fouche. "There was no mention of this in your report."

"Excellency, we didn't feel that it was that important to tell you at this time since we are aware that the mountain is becoming more stable."

"Tell it like it is, Mayor" Father Roche yelled.

"Don't yell at me, Father Roche!" retorted the Mayor.

"Gentlemen, let us be calm. Just tell me what's happening in St. Pierre," said the Governor.

"Excellency, I can assure you that despite the unfortunate happenings of today, I believe we have seen the worst of the mountain." said Mayor Fouche."

"Well, gentlemen." said the Governor with sarcasm in his voice. "We will know if there is anymore cause for alarm if the mountain erupts and buries the lot of you in the next day or so, won't we?"

The others laughed at the Governor's feeble effort to put sarcastic humor into the meeting.

"What's the situation about this small pox?"

"Well, Sir," said the Mayor. "I think that we will have that problem licked."

"Do you have enough vaccine?" asked the Governor.

"I believe so," replied the Mayor.

Father Mary turned to the others and said, "I think you have not taken this situation seriously, gentlemen."

"What do you mean?" asked the Governor.

"Do you know how many persons have been killed in the last four days, Excellency?"

The Governor thought for a few seconds then said. "A hundred, perhaps two hundred."

"The count was over six hundred before we came here this evening. It may be more when we return to Saint Pierre." said Father Mary.

"Nonsense!" retorted Mayor Fouche. "That is sheer nonsense, Father Mary."

"I took the precaution of checking with our church records and those of the hospital and those figures given to me, total over six hundred and this doesn't take into consideration of the many who were washed out to sea or buried by the mud."

It seems, Father Mary," said the Governor, "that you have been talking about the danger and the loss of so many. Perhaps you can tell me what I should do."

Evacuate all of Saint Pierre and the surrounding communities immediately." replied Father Mary.

We couldn't do that, Father Mary," said Governor Mouttet. "There is an election taking place very shortly. It would disrupt the proceedings and the election would have to be called off."

If the volcano erupts, the elections won't be the only thing that is disrupted, Excellency."

"I don't think that there is that much cause for alarm, Father. In fact to assure you of my feeling of wellbeing of everyone in that city, I will personally go into Saint Pierre the day after tomorrow. I am sure that my presence will calm any fears that the townspeople may have and dispel any desires to evacuate the city."

"Your presence in our city will do a great deal to relieve all of us, Excellency," said Mayor Fouche."

"Good!" said Governor Mouttet. "Perhaps Mayor Fouche, you would be so kind as to arrange for Madame Mouttet and I to stay at the Hotel de L'Independance while we are there. You might also advise the Vicar General that we will attend Mass in the Cathedral on Thursday morning. I am sure that when the general populace see us there, it will act as the catalyst needed to instill calm amongst them."

"Yes, of course, Excellency." replied the Mayor who visibly showed signs of gratefulness to the governor as he bowed slightly towards the governor.

"Well, Gentlemen, if there is nothing more for you to discuss, then I suggest that we adjourn this meeting so that you may return to Saint Pierre," said the Governor.

Everyone left the room with their own thoughts and climbed into the carriages that brought them to Fort du France.

Marcel Hayot called out to Father Mary. "Father, would you like to return to St Pierre in my carriage?"

"Thank you very much," replied the priest as he climbed into the carriage.The carriage raced along the road towards St. Pierre, as there were rumors that some Voodoo cultists were attacking travelers along the road between the two cities.

"You didn't say much at the meeting Marcel."

"No, Father Mary, I didn't, but you expressed my sentiments very well."

"I am glad someone listened."

"I know Mister Prentiss, the American Consul quite well, and tomorrow I am going to meet with him for lunch and see if I can talk him into sending a letter to his President."

"A letter to the President of the United States?"

"Yes, perhaps the President can persuade the Governor to evacuate the city. If not, perhaps the President can persuade the Minister of the colonies to order the Governor to evacuate."

"A good idea, Marcel," said Father Roche. "Incidentally, what's this I hear about Rachelle and the young doctor?"

"I am afraid that they have broken off their engagement, Father."

"I was afraid of that, Marcel. I had so wanted to marry the two of them."

"It was my wish also, Father Mary."

The two then continued on in silence as the carriage sped towards the city.

Chapter Fifteen

Suddenly at the outskirts of the city, both men heard a loud explosion from the direction of Mt. Pelee and then looked up at the volcano. Long tongues of flames shot upwards into the sky. The light from the flames reflected a red glow from the overhanging clouds onto the city and countryside below. The ground shook and the horses frightened by the shaking ground beneath their feet, sped on in a greater frenzy. Soon the sky turned a bright orange as yellow sheets of flames shot out of the crater followed by arcs of reddish-orange lava shooting over the lip of the crater and down the side of the mountain. Within minutes, the entire topmost part of the crater was a fiery orange and the two men looked on in terror as the orange lava began to slowly descend down the mountain.

Andre and Monique had been in the middle of an embrace, while lying half asleep on her bed when the loud deafening explosion from Pelee startled them.

"It's just another of Pelee's way of being a damned nuisance." said Andre angrily as he sat up in the bed.

"But Andre," said Monique as she too sat up. "it could be a real eruption this time." She was undoubtedly alarmed and that alarm was apparent to Andre.

The entire room lit up a faint orange colour as the reflection from the lava spewing out of the volcano began its descent down the mountain. The couple ran to the window facing Pelee.

"God! Saints protect us! I can't believe it." exclaimed Andre. "I have never seen anything like it."

"Neither have I." replied Monique as she stared at the volcano as if hypnotized.

The top of the Pelee was a glowing bright orange and as the lava moved down the ravines of the peak, it turned red. Two bright orange streams of lava poured down the mountain at a faster speed than the red streams as the lava steams were heading straight towards St. Pierre. Outside, there was panic in the streets. Andre opened the door slightly and heard voices crying out. "Run for your lives! Run to the waterfront!"

"We had better get dressed." said Monique as she pulled Andre from the slightly opened door.

Both got dressed and went outdoors and joined the crowd heading towards the waterfront. Panic was everywhere. How ironic it seemed to Andre that only less than twelve hours earlier the populace was running away from the sea and towards the mountain to escape the huge wave heading towards the city.

When they reached the waterfront, many of the people stood in the water up to their necks in hope that the lava would stop at the shoreline.

"This is ridiculous!" Andre shouted above the din to Monique.

"Why?"

"The lava couldn't be that close to the city. It would take half a day to reach the city. Let's go back to your place."

"But Andre," said Monique, I am not sure if it would be a wise thing to do."

"Then let's climb up the hill overlooking the city and from there we can see the lava flow."

"I'm not sure if—."

Andre interjected, "Believe me, we would be a lot safer on the hill. Lava doesn't run up a hill."

"You're right," said Monique. "Come on. I know a short cut up the hill."

The two fought their way through the frightened crowd and soon were climbing a deserted path leading up the hill. When they finally reached the summit, they stared at the volcano ahead of them that was few kilometres away. The two lava streams were only a kilometre down the slopes of the volcano and were heading down two ravines that would bypass the city. The streams moved slowly down the mountain, burning the trees in their way. The volcano meanwhile constantly roared through its new ordeal.

Andre and Monique stood on the hill for an hour, and then decided that it would be safe to go back to her house. Many of the town's people who had climbed the hill to get a better view of the volcano, reached a similar conclusion and by three in the morning, the hill and the waterfront were both empty.

The volcano continued to spew out lava, and flames shot upwards of a thousand metres. The entire countryside was red from the reflections of the flames, and the grayish-white ash mantle covering everything had a distinctive reddish tint. The low overhanging clouds of smoke occasionally reflected the flames, giving the clouds a reddish-brown hue.

Andre and Monique had reached her house without incident and in a few minutes, they were back in bed. Andre had been asleep for another hour before he was wakened up again, this time by shouts in the street. He stood at the window and looked towards the mountain and could still see the reddish brown sky. But what concerned him most were the red hot cinders that seemed to be falling everywhere. He went to the front door and opened it. Outside, he could see the cinders falling like glowing red snow flakes. Many of the cinders continued to smolder after they had settled on the ground and the roofs of the houses.

Down the street, about three houses away, a small crowd had gathered in front of one of the houses. Judging from the bright orange reflections on the faces of the crowd, Andre assumed that the house was on fire.

"Monique!" yelled Andre. "You had better get dressed." Andre walked towards the bed and then shook the sleeping form in it.

Monique stirred, then mumbled, "What's wrong, Andre?"

"I think the house down the street is on fire."

"Oh no!' exclaimed Monique as she jumped out of bed.

Within minutes the two of them were dressed and outside. From the shouts of the crowd, Andre suspected that there was no chance that the house could be saved. The flames began shooting across the street, splitting the crowd into two groups.

"Is there anyone inside?" asked Andre of a man nearby.

"No!" yelled the spectator. "They all got outside, but I think there is an old woman in the house next door."

Andre looked at the house that the spectator was pointing to and cried out, "If she isn't brought out of there soon, she will die in the flames."

The house that the old woman was in was beginning to burn on the side facing the burning house.

"Why doesn't someone go in and bring her out?" yelled Andre.

"It would take two men." replied a large man looking towards the house. "She is very heavy and I can't find another to help me."

"You have now!" yelled Andre, "Show me the way."

"Be careful Andre," added Monique.

"I will, I will."

The two men crossed the street and after ducking a few bursts of flames from the inferno next door, they managed to get into the house which was by now filling with dense smoke.

"Let's close the front door!" yelled Andre. "Otherwise it will create a draft that will suck the flames into the house."

The other man closed the door behind him. With the door closed the house became darkened with the exception of a slight reddish glow at the back of the house.

"Do you think the fire has reached any of the rooms back there?" asked Andre.

"I'll look," replied the other.

The other man went to the back of the house and then returned. "That glow is from the fire next door. I think the heat will break the window in a few moments so we better get the woman out of here."

"OK," replied Andre, "but where is she?"

The two men went back to the front of the house, and then climbed the stairs.

When they reached the second floor, they could see flames and smoke coming into the house from one of the rooms at the rear of the house. The two men opened one of the doors and stepped into the room where the old woman was sleeping.

"Woman!" yelled Andre "Get out of your bed! Your house is on fire."

The woman moaned, "I can't. I am crippled."

The two men headed towards the woman's bed. Andre noticed that there was a slight reddish glow in the area of the drapes and just as he was going to draw them open, he heard a splintering sound down stairs. The heat of the fire next door had broken the side window.

"Oh! Oh!" yelled the other man. "If we don't get out of here soon, we'll be trapped."

The two men tried to move the old woman who was quite fat but couldn't move her because of her weight. Andre could hear the roar of fire downstairs and struggled to pull the woman out of bed. Finally the woman toppled to the floor. When the two men tried to get her on her feet, she fell to the floor again.

"We'll have to drag her out of the house," said Andre as he yanked a blanket off the bed.

The two men rolled the woman onto the blanket which Andre had placed on the floor and then began pulling the blanket and the old woman across the floor. Just as they reached the door to the hallway, the bedroom window burst from the heat and glass shattered into the closed drapes. The drapes began burning and within seconds, dark smoke began filling up the room. As they approached the stairs, they could see the fire and smoke swirling its way up the stairs.

"We will have to drag her down the stairs if we want to get out of her alive." Andre said to the other man.

The two men began dragging the hysterical woman down the stairs oblivious of the fact that her head was rebounding off the steps. By the time they reached the main floor, the stairs were burning furiously. The ceiling above them was in flames and the heat was becoming more intense every moment. The two men continued pulling on the blanket and were soon dragging the woman through the main entrance. Within a few seconds, the three of them were outside gasping for the fresh air that awaited them. There was a great cheer from the crowd when the two men were seen emerging from the doorway with the old woman.

Monique ran over to Andre and hugged him tightly and cried, "I thought you would never get out, Andre!"

"So did I." answered Andre with a smile. Andre and Monique walked back to her house down the street.

"It seems that the cinders coming out of the mountain are not as numerous as before," remarked Andre with the relief showing on his face as he looked towards the mountain.

"They eased up when you were in the house," answered Monique.

The two of them, hand in hand, stepped inside Monique's house, oblivious of the fact that there where other houses in the city that caught fire.

Four hundred kilometres to the north, the Quebec Line steamboat *Roraima* bound for Demerara, British Guiana via the Windward Islands was steaming through calm seas. At her present course and speed, the 2,712 tonne schooner would arrive at her next port of call, Dominica in the early hours of Thursday.

Captain Muggah approached Ellery Scott, his First Mate on the bridge. "Can you see through the fog?"

"It's pretty thick, Sir." replied the Mate. "I've noticed it since dawn this morning. At first I thought that it would go away but we have been in it for several hours."

"I don't think its fog at all, Mr. Scott. I think were steaming through smoke of some kind. Best reduce the speed, Mr. Scott, lest we hit another boat."

"Aye, Sir," replied Mr. Scott as he turned to relay the Captain's orders to the helmsman.

The captain began thinking to himself about the smoke and was considering the source when he heard the Mate calling him.

"Captain!"

The captain turned around and saw Mr. Scott approaching him. The mate then said, "If we decrease our speed, we may not arrive until the afternoon of Thursday and you know how hot those afternoons are. Could we not maintain our present speed? If we do, we will arrive in St. Pierre in the early morning when it's still cool."

"Yes. I realize that discharging cargo in the afternoon is a difficult task but there is nothing else I can do but to reduce the speed. I don't want to hit another ship in this smoke." replied the captain.

"Do you have any idea where the smoke is coming from?" asked the Mate.

"Soufriere."

"Beg your pardon?"

"The smoke is probably from the volcano on the island of Saint Vincent. The volcano is called Soufriere."

"How do you know it's coming from Soufriere, Sir?"

"I heard a report at the last city we stopped at, that Soufriere is acting up."

"Thank God. The closest we will be to that volcano is Martinique." said Mr. Scott.

"Yes," added the captain. "At least Mount Pelee is a dead volcano."

"Dormant is a word I believe that they use." said Mr. Scott as both men laughed.

"You know, the last time Soufriere acted up, was a little over a year ago. Prior to that, the volcano was dormant."

"What happened when it erupted?" asked the Mate.

"Nothing much," replied the captain, "There was a series of sharp tremors through the northern part of the island which frightened many of the Carib settlements. For the next ten months, earthquakes hit the island but most of the whites really weren't concerned because earthquakes around these islands are nothing new to them."

"So now you think its erupting then." said the Mate.

"I don't know," replied the captain, "but on April 14th, there was a series of shocks felt around the island and a number of landslides prevailed that night from the slopes of Soufriere."

"Will we have to stop off at Saint Vincent on our return trip to France?"

"No," replied the captain. "We will sail directly from British Guiana to France."

The air within the walls of the prison in St. Pierre was hot and stuffy. Rumors had circulated around the prison that the day had arrived that the ringleaders would be punished for the riot of several days back.

Ciparis looked out of the tiny window of his cell and could see a number of trusties bringing out the apparatus for the whipping of those to be punished. They raised the plank onto two blocks of wood. The plank was less than a metre off the ground. The plank, being half a metre wide and two metres long, was a formidable looking instrument of punishment and yet, this was only half of the apparatus. The other half was by far the worst. It was a smaller version of the English cat-o'-nine tails. As its younger brother, it had only six tails with each tail being seven and a half millimetres in thickness and four hundred and fifty millimetres in length. It was attached to a wooden handle. The men to be punished would be stripped and laid out on the plank which was called the 'Justice Bench' and whipped across their bare backs. The victim's feet and hands would be secured to the iron rings attached to the blocks of wood. Many times, Ciparis had seen this punishment given. He also saw many of them die on the plank.

The Governor of the prison being a huge man, walked across the prison yard with steadiness in his gait followed by fifteen armed guards and the same number of trusties who held club-like weapons in their hands. They disappeared into one of the entrances leading into one of the buildings. Down a dark and slippery stairway they went until they were almost enveloped in darkness. The party of men reached a cell which had been used to house the five ring leaders who were to be whipped. The door was opened and the governor of the prison followed several of the armed guards into the cell. The condemned were made to stand up against the wall.

The governor began. "You five men were the ringleaders of the riot the other day and as such, I have decided on your punishment. Each of you will receive fifty strokes of the whip on your bare backs,"

"No! No!" screamed one of the men. "You can't do this to me!"

One of guards struck the man in the stomach with a rifle. The governor snarled. "Let me say this once and for all so that there will be no misunderstanding. My decision is final and as such you will conduct yourselves as men. If we have to drag any of you out of here, that person will receive an additional fifty strokes and I don't have to tell you what that will mean.

Some of the men began to cry, others prayed for mercy.

"Take them out!" yelled the governor.

The trusties ran towards the men and began to shove them out of the cell.

"Look out" yelled one of the trustees, "One of them is running away!"

One of the five prisoners disappeared into the darkness of the hallway and soon a number of guards and trustees began to follow him.

"Don't shoot him!" ordered the governor. "I want him alive so he can die on the Justice Bench."

The party of condemned men accompanied by the governor, the guards and trustees stepped out into the bright daylight and squinted their eyes to shield out the glaring light. Within a few moments, four of the condemned men were sitting down on the ground facing the 'Justice Bench.'

Less than a minute later the fifth man who ran away was brought out. His screams could be heard throughout the prison. He was dragged towards the "Justice Bench." He broke away and prostrated himself before the governor.

"Please Sir." begged the man. "Just give me the fifty like the others. I don't want to die."

The governor made no reply but motioned to the trustees to prepare him. The trustees grabbed the man and stripped him of his clothes and laid the wretched man on the plank. As soon as his hands and his feet were secured, one of the trusties took his shirt off and reached into a bag. He pulled out the whip and flicked it in the air with a resounding snap which echoed off the walls of the prison.

While this was going on, the other four were ordered to strip. When the others were stripped and made to sit down again, the trustee, a huge man with rippling muscles, flicked the whip again.

The governor spoke in loud clear tones, "You will all witness the punishment that these five men are going to receive. In future, anyone who riots again, will receive one hundred strokes of the whip that this man is going to receive."

The governor of the prison motioned to the trusty with the whip to commence carrying out the sentence. The trustee lifted the whip high into the air and swinging it around his head three times, he brought it down on the back of the man on the plank. The cords of the whip dug deep into the flesh of the man and turned red as the cords were dragged through the man's bleeding flesh. One of the guards wrote on a piece of paper, the number one and yelled out, "One!"

The trustee again raised his arm and the whip followed suit and again it was whirled about the trustee's head, then he brought it down on the back of the victim.

"There is no need to withhold your screaming," said the governor rather sarcastically to the condemned man. There is no doubt in my mind that you won't survive the hundred so have no fear. You won't have to live with the shame."

"You pig!" yelled the man in reply.

"Pigs squeal," replied the governor, "and like all pigs, you will squeal. I venture to say that we will get you squealing before the fifty is reached. And before seventy-five is reached, we hear you curse your mother for having given birth to you."

"You will hear nothing but oaths of damnation aimed at you, you filthy pig," answered the man.

The governor motioned to the trustee and again the whip was brought down on the man's back.

"Three!" yelled the guard.

The governor leaned towards the condemned man and sneered in a soft voice. "I think you may even be silent forever after seventy-five is reached." When twenty-five strokes had been administered, the trustee handed the whip to another who immediately brought the instrument of torture down on the back of the groaning man on the plank. The governor stood beside the condemned man and again spoke softly. "Don't you feel better now that you have had some of the evil beaten out of you?"

The man made no reply but glared at the fat face that scorned him. When fifty strokes had been reached, the man was screaming to the obvious glee of the governor.

"I told you that you would squeal like a pig." the governor laughed haughtily.

The trustee handed the whip back to the first trustee who commenced, with the fifty-first stroke. As the governor had predicted, the screaming had stopped at approximately seventy-five and all that could be heard was low moaning noises from the condemned man.

At eighty-five, one of the guards grabbed the condemned man's wrist to feel for the pulse.

"He's dead sir."

The governor looked down at the bleeding form before him and then remarked. "When I order one hundred strokes, that is what he receives. Continue with the whipping."

Some of the others of the condemned began to vomit in utter fear. One of the men couldn't take the strain any longer so in an instant, he leaped up and dashed towards the main entrance in the desperate hope of escaping. He was caught in less than a minute and dragged screaming towards the centre of the yard.

"It seems that we have another man who wishes to die," laughed the governor.

After the hundredth stroke of the whip had been administered to the first man, his body was taken off of the plank and dragged along the ground to a small hut where the bodies of dead prisoners were kept prior to burial. The second man was dragged to the 'Justice Plank' and the whipping commenced as soon as he was secured to the iron rings. As the first stroke of the hundred was being administered to the second condemned man, the governor snarled at the remaining three quivering prisoners. "Perhaps, some of you would like to receive an extra fifty. If so, do what these two fools did and you can join them in Hell."

As one of the guards called out the strokes, the men in the prison yard flinched at each stroke. Ciparis couldn't look anymore so he sat down on his pile of straw. But the sound of the whip cracking down on the naked flesh of the victim was more than he could take so he stuck his fingers in his ears to block out the victim's screams. It didn't really help that much.

Chapter Sixteen

Fernand Clerc reached the offices of the Mayor Fouche and after waiting for half an hour, he was invited into the mayor's inner office.

"Fernand!" said the mayor. "Please come in, my good man." The two men shook hands and Fouche offered Clerc a chair.

"What's on your mind, this fine morning?" asked the Mayor. Then he answered his own question. "Oh yes. The volcano. It was quite a fireworks display we had last night but the fires were put out."

"Mayor Fouche," began Clerc. "How long do you intend to keep the public misinformed about the true situation of the pending disaster?" "Nonsense!" retorted the Mayor. "Disaster, be damned. Certainly, we have had some difficulties but it is apparent that the worst is over."

"You said that a few day ago, your worship, but each day has got worse."

"That's true, but I have it from good authority that the volcanic activity is on the wane."

"Good authority, eh? You mean, professor Landes. You may believe that botanist but I for one don't"

"Sir," replied Mayor Fouche, "I have a great deal of respect for our professor and more importantly, I believe him."

"Mayor Fouche. Are you intending to withhold any orders to the soldiers for the populace to evacuate Saint Pierre?"

"Yes! That is so. I do not intend to order the city to evacuate. I don't think that the situation merits it."

"What in your mind do you consider a serious enough situation that would merit the evacuation of the city?"

Obviously, if lava poured into the city, this would in my mind constitute an emergency."

"If poisonous gas were descending upon the city, would you consider evacuation of the city?"

"Is poisonous gas descending upon the city?"

"No."

"Then when it does, I will consider that problem then. And now Sir, I must ask you to let me be as I have much work to do. "Fernand Clerc left the office of the Mayor with his face flushed in anger. He knew that the mayor couldn't evacuate the city in time if poisonous gasses blew into the city. Clerc drove to the Cathedral to discuss the situation with the Vicar-General of the island. Perhaps, he could use his influence to persuade the governor in Fort de France to bring about an evacuation of the city. "But Monsieur Clerc," remarked Gabriel Parel, who was the Vicar-General. "I understand your concern, but surely you appreciate my position also. I am merely a priest, attempting to comfort his flock."

"You are the Vicar-General and as such, you have considerable influence on this island."

"Perhaps, but I cannot use my influence to go against the authority of the mayor."

"Suppose the wishes of the mayor are not to the best interests of the populace?"

"Then, Sir, the people will have to vote themselves a new mayor, won't they."

"I believe," said Clerc, "that you are attempting to remain aloof to the dangers of the volcano."

"Perhaps that is so, Monsieur Clerc, however I can assure you that when the governor or for that matter, even the Mayor of Saint Pierre orders the city to evacuate, I shall give such an order my utmost blessing and instruct my flock to obey the order instantly."

"I certainly hope, Vicar-General, that when the order is finally given, there will still be members of your flock alive to obey them."

Clerc then left and went to the office of Andreus Hurard, the editor of the newspaper.

"Monsieur Hurard, I have come to discuss the evacuation of St. Pierre." "You mean the governor has ordered it?"

"No! But I think he may, if he is convinced of the dangers pending."

"I doubt very much if he is concerned about any immediate dangers that are imminent."

"I seem to remember his lack of concern yesterday and since then we have lost hundreds of lives."

"Yes, that is unfortunate, Monsieur Clerc, but I believe that we have seen the end of Pelee's fury!"

"How can you be sure of that?"

"Professor Landes has advised me of this."

"Is the professor an authority on volcanology?"

The editor paused then replied, "No, but I respect him as a professor."

"Yes, as a professor of botany, but not as a volcanologist."

"There is no volcanologist on this island, so I look to the professor for advice."

"If you had a pain in your belly and there was no medical doctor on the island, would you look to the professor for advice as to whether your appendix should be removed?"

The editor sneered, "I am a busy man, Monsieur Clerc, so I must ask you to leave me be. Good day, Sir!"

Clerc realized that it was pointless to discuss anything further with the editor, so without another word, he left his office. He realized that only the governor could have the final say and even though he knew there was little chance that the governor would co-operate, but despite his doubts, he decided to give it a try.

An hour later, he was in Fort Du France and at the governor's mansion. "The governor will see you now, Monsieur Clerc," said the assistant. Clerc was led into the office of the Governor Mouttet. "Monsieur Clerc! What brings you to Fort Du France?"

"Your Excellency, I have come to plead with you to reconsider the evacuation of St. Pierre."

"But Monsieur Clerc, surely you remember in our meeting last night, this matter was discussed and it was decided that there wasn't an imminent need to evacuate. In fact Professor Landes more or less assured us that Pelee's fury was on the wane."

"Yes, I remember but I was not in accord with his report, as you may remember."

"That's true but the final decision is mine and I said that I would abide by the consensus of the committee of which you yourself are a member. "Clerc shifted uneasily in his chair because he knew the governor was right on that point. Then he said. "Sir, wouldn't it be safer to evacuate the city for at least a few days until we can be sure of what Pelee is going to do?

"The governor realized that he may have to give such an order but needed time to stall, at least until the Progressive Party was assured of a victory. "Monsieur Clerc, he began, "I can assure you that I will give this matter my deepest consideration. Let me suggest a compromise. I plan to attend the festivities in Saint Pierre on the eighth so if the situation hasn't improved by then, I will order the evacuation by the ninth."

"Thank you very much, Your Excellency, for at least reconsidering the possibility of an evacuation. I sincerely hope that we will all still be around by the eighth."

"Well," said the Governor with a smile. "If it's any comfort to you, you know that if I personally thought that Pelee was going to explode by the eighth, there is no way that I would venture inside St. Pierre under any circumstances. Surely my willingness to go to St. Pierre under these circumstances, should remove any immediate fears you may have about an imminent eruption, am I right?"

"Sir," answered Clerc, "Your presence in the city will convince me that you are convinced of the safety in the city, even if I am not."

Rene Rousseau had called a meeting of the leaders of the Island's Voodoo cultists for the late afternoon. They had decided to meet in an abandoned house a few kilometres east of St. Pierre.

"It is important that we decide on our course of action." Rene said to the others sitting around him.

"I'm not sure if the plan you have in mind is the right one we should carry out," remarked one of the cultists.

"Why not?" asked Rene angrily.

"Because it involves wholesale murder."

"Are you afraid to commit murder?"

"No, of course not, but if we are going to kill all the island's leaders, we must be sure that all of them are killed, and that there are no survivors left to hunt us down."

"That's true," added another.

Rene turned looked out one of the windows then said, "I agree that we must kill all of them if we are to succeed."

"What's the purpose of killing the leaders of the island?" asked a small man whom the others called Leon.

Rene turned abruptly and faced Leon and demanded, "Do you want the whites to rule us forever?"

"No. But surely there must be some other way?"

"There is none," replied Rene, "And now, I will present you with the names of those who are to die."

The men shuffled uneasily waiting for the list of the doomed men.

"The Governor?" one managed to gasp.

"He is number one on the list." replied Rene. "And number two is the Deputy Governor."

The men eyed each other with bewilderment at Rene's ambitious plans.

"Senator Knight is number three."

"But," stammered one of the men, "he is black like the rest of us."

"That is true," replied Rena, "but he must die because he is a member of the Chamber of Deputies. He will be looked to as the leader if all the major white leaders are killed. If that happens, he will eradicate Voodooism. With him, there will be no peace for Voodoo cultists like ourselves.

The man who doubted the wisdom of such a move against Senator Knight, nodded his approval.

"Mayor Fouche is next."

"Yes." murmured a few of the men.

"The Military Commander in Saint Pierre," remarked Rene and then with a smile, "The same goes for the Military Commander in Fort du France."

"What about the governor of the military prison in St. Pierre?" asked one of the men who began reaching around his back to scratch the scars that crisscrossed his back.

"Yes, of course," replied Rene. "and also Father Mary in Morne Rouge."

"A priest?" asked one with a startled voice.

"Yes, a priest. This man must surely die for he is the island's most outspoken critic on Voodooism."

"If we are going to kill a priest, then we had best kill the Vicar-General also for he will rally the people when he finds out what we are up to." remarked one of the men.

One of the men spoke, "I think that you had best add the name of Andreus Hurard, the editor of "Les Colonies."

"Why?" asked another of the men,

"Because," replied the first, "this man can sway the people to fight against us."

"Or join us." remarked another.

"He dies!" said Rene with finality in his voice.

"Alfred Percin will have to go also," said one of men.

"Yes!" said Rene. "He is an active member of the political field and as such would be looked on as a leader.

"What about Professor Landers?" asked one of the men.

"What about him?"

"Well he seems to be a leader."

"Forget him," said Rene. "He is a nothing."

"Well," said Leon, "are there any more?"

"Yes, two more," replied Rene. "but neither of these are leaders in the community."

"Who are they?" asked one of the men.

"One is a young doctor called Andre Verlaine who has taken it upon himself to sleep with a mulato girl."

"Yes!" added one of the men. "Both the doctor and the girl should be killed.

"No!" exclaimed Rene. "Not the girl."

"Why not?" asked one of the cultists.

"Because, she is my sister."

The men eyed each other then one of them spoke and said. "Very well, Rene, we will kill only the doctor but you will have to point him out to us. "One of the other men then asked, "Who is the other person who has to be killed."

Rene looked about the room then said, "There is a traitor amongst us."

"Impossible!" yelled Leon.

"It is true," added Rene.

"How do you know?" asked another.

"I found out from one of my own informants."

"Who is it?"

Rene smiled and then said. "I have a little game for all of us to play. When the game is over, you will see for yourselves."

"Games! Games!" remarked Leon angrily.

"Who ever heard of playing games like this?"

Rene pulled out a revolver and spoke, "I will order all of you to close your eyes and I also will close mine. The traitor will have thirty seconds to escape. I promise that for thirty seconds, he can escape unharmed. After that, we will chase him. We may catch him or he may really escape. It's a gamble. It's a game."

"What happens if after thirty seconds, he is still with us?" asked Leon.

"Then I will point him out to you after I have counted thirty-one and will present my proof of his guilt to you."

"How can you be so sure? You could be wrong." remarked Leon.

"I am not wrong," sneered Rene as he squinted his eyes.

"When does your game begin?" asked one of men.

"Now!" yelled Rene. "Close your eyes."

All the men closed their eyes and Rene began counting. "One, two, three." At four, he also closed his eyes. When he reached twenty, he heard a shuffling noise but kept his eyes closed tight despite the temptation to see who was moving about.

"Twenty-nine, thirty." Rene opened his eyes and ordered the others to open their eyes also.

"Well," said Rene, the traitor has flown the coop."

"Leon!" yelled several of the men at once.

"After him." ordered Rene. "I want him alive."

The men leaped up and scrambled outside to catch the fleeing quarry.

Within minutes, Leon was captured and brought before Rene.

"Who told you it is me?" asked Leon.

"No one."

"But what made you think it is me?"

"All my informant told me was that I had a traitor in our group. He didn't know the name."

"It isn't me. Please you must believe me."

"Then why did you run?" asked one of the men.

"It was the way he looked at me." replied Leon.

"Not good enough, Leon." remarked Rene. "You must die for betraying us. If you had remained in the room we never would have known. Bind his hands and feet!"

"Have mercy," pleaded Leon.

The men tied Leon's hands and feet together.

"You are going to be an example to my men as to what happens to traitors." said Rene as he reached behind a table and pulled out a heavy axe handle.

"What are you going to do to me?"

"This!" exclaimed Rene as he brought the heavy club across the shin bones of Leon's right leg. Leon screamed in pain.

"I want this man—this pig, beaten to death. Before he dies, every bone in his body must be broken."

"Mercy, Rene!" pleaded Leon.

"You will be given mercy, you pig, when every bone of your body is broken, not before." Rene turned to one of his leaders and said, "Make sure he is buried deep when you are finished with him."

"Yes, Rene. It shall be done," replied the other man.

Rene motioned to one of the other men next to him to follow him amidst the screams of Leon as he was being systematically beaten to death by his former friends.

"I want you to keep an eye on my sister and report to me if the doctor shows up at her house or at the cabaret."

The other man nodded in the affirmative as they continued to walk down the path leading through the forest. Behind them, they could hear the screams of the dying cultist.

It was about two in the afternoon when Andre left Monique's house. He planned to visit Father Mary in the village of Morne Rouge. As he walked through the mud in the streets, he felt sick to his stomach. In some places, the muck was a combination of ash, dead animals, excrement, and grey mud. To fall in it was the same as being buried in it. In less than a block, Andre was covered all over his body with the foul smelling muck.

Twice, he vomited, the stench was so bad. Suddenly, he heard a thunderous roar and one glance at Pelee told him that there was more to expect. Large billows of black smoke shot out of the volcano and rose upwards. Within a few minutes, the sky was overcast, and as before, the day slowly began to turn into night. In less than five minutes, the dark cloud had descended over the countryside and the city was enveloped in complete darkness. For over an hour, he struggled up the streets to the outskirts of the city and by some miracle, he found his way to the road that led to the village of Morne Rouge.

It wasn't until five in the afternoon that Andre reached the doors of the Church in Morne Rouge.

Father Mary opened the door and looked at the muddy form. "It's me, Andre Verlaine." cried out Andre.

"Come in, my boy." said the priest.

Andre shuffled into the entrance of the church and after the door was shut behind him, Father Mary said, "It's a miracle you found your way in this darkness."

"To be true, it is," replied Andre. "Please, could I have some water?"

"Of course! of course! Follow me." replied the priest as he led Andre through a series of doors until they were in the priest's private quarters.

"What brings you to Marne Rouge?" asked the priest as he handed Andre a cup of water.

"I have come to ask your advice about Voodooism. I understand you are the island's leading authority on it."

"Leading critic is probably the best term to use," replied Father Mary, "But why do you want to know about Voodooism"

"A very good friend of mine has a brother whom I believe practices Voodooism."

"You are speaking of Rene Rousseau, aren't you?"

"How did you know that?"

"There isn't much that goes on in this island that I don't know. Monique is a very delightful girl but are you sure this is the girl you want?"

"Yes, I think she is but I want to know about this Voodooism because of her brother's involvement in it."

"You can rest assured my son; that Monique doesn't believe in that sort of stuff."

"Yes, I know."

"Well, I will attempt to describe Voodooism to you," continued the priest. "It's a folk religion that is practiced mainly in Haiti. It combines many of the elements of the Catholic religion with many of the African tribal beliefs. A great importance is given to three groups of the spirits. The saints, the dead and the twins. Of these, the saints have attracted the greatest interest because many of them represent an identification of various Catholic saints with African tribal deities. Saint Patrick, for example is identified with the Dohomean snake deity Damballah, Saint James the Elder with Ogism, the Yoruba deity of iron and warfare. The list is endless.

"Do they have a ritual?" asked Andre.

"There are many rituals," replied the priest. "Often families will perform a ritual, or gather collectively and sometimes communities perform a single ritual. As I mentioned, the rituals are also based on many of the Catholics elements such as our Hail Mary, the Lords

Prayer, the practice of making the sign of the cross, baptism and the use of bells."

"I have heard drums often at night in the distance."

"Drums. Ah yes, drums. Every ritual has its drums. There is much drumming and singing during the rituals."

Andre looked outside and noticed that the sky was beginning to clear up. Then he asked, "What about the killing of animals?"

"Well as a rule, services for the saints or twins often involves a feast and a dance."

"Is it true that during the feast, the cultists engage in cannibalism? asked Andre.

"I have never known of such cases of cannibalism or human sacrifice being used as an element for a ritual although persons have been murdered in the name of Voodoo. Usually a chicken, or a goat, or a pig or even a bullock is ceremonially killed and eaten. Often during a ceremony, one or more cultist will dance to the rhythm of a special saint. Each saint has a special drum beat. These dancers get so involved in their dance, that they often have no memory of the ceremony after it's over."

"Is there any truth about Voodoo priests being able to cast spells on their victims?"

"I am not sure," replied the priest. "You know that more things are wrought from Heaven and Earth by prayer, or so the biblical quotation says. I think that the converse may be held to be true when it comes to cursing someone. After all, what is a curse but a form of prayer?"

There was a knock on the door, and a little old man opened the door. "Father, someone is in the church to see you."

"Thank you. Tell him I will be right out." Father Mary turned to Andre and said, "Please excuse me for a few minutes."

"Yes, Father, of course."

The priest was gone for fifteen minutes, then returned. He looked ashen-faced when he spoke to Andre. "Andre, I have just talked with an informer with the Voodoo cultists. Rene Rouseau has advised his band that they intend to kill the island's leaders."

"Why?"

"They want to take over the island."

"But that would be impossible."

"Not if they kill the leaders of the island. But what they don't know is that the French warship *Suchet* in the harbour would report the event to Paris.

"Are you going to send the informer to warn the Governor?"

"No, he has risked enough. He says that Rene already knew that there was an informer in his midst and ordered the killing of one of his men. The wrong one."

"I will warn the governor then." said Andre.

"No. It would be better if I warn him through the Vicar-General." I will say that I learned of the plot in the confessional. This way, I can protect the informer."

"Can I help?"

"Yes, watch out for yourself because you have been marked for death also by Rene."

"Why?"

"Because of your love for Monique."

"Has he any plans for her?"

"None that I was able to determine from my talk with the traitor." replied the priest. "Incidentally, there is one thing you can do for me."

"What is it, Father?"

"There is the chance that I might be killed before I get to Fort du France to warn the Vicar-General."

"You? Why?"

"I am also on the list because of my outspoken views on Voodooism."

"What can I do for you?" asked Andre.

Speak with Monsieur Clerc, tomorrow. If he hasn't heard of the plot, then it means that I haven't been able to pass the information on to the Vicar-General."

"We better leave now," said Andre.

"No." replied the priest. "We had better wait around until dark just in case some of the cultists are waiting around."

"Yes, perhaps you are right."

"Then join me for supper." smiled Father Mary.

The two men got up and went into the kitchen to prepare what might be their last supper.

but he could still hear and feel the rumblings inside of the volcano.

The Governor of the island was looking out of his window when he heard footsteps behind him.

"Governor."

He recognized the voice of the Lieutenant-Governor and turned and said, "You know, Edward, I am not sure about the state of the affairs in Saint Pierre."

"What do you mean, Sir?"

"I received a visit from the Editor of Les Colonies and it seems that our strong supporter is going over to the other side."

"Politically?"

"No! What I mean he says he has had some second thoughts about the evacuation of Saint Pierre."

"So have I, Sir." added L"Heurre.

"You too?"

"Yes Sir. I think the volcano will explode and wipe out the entire city in the next few days."

"Well, I was planning to visit the city on the eighth to study the situation but I have decided to go tomorrow instead," smiled the governor.

The Lieutenant-Governor shuffled uneasily, then remarked, "I suppose you will want me to accompany you."

"No. You can remain behind until I return." Then the governor picked up some papers and after looking at them for a minute, he said, "I now want to discuss with you the execution of the condemned rapist, Ciparis."

"Are you still planning to have him executed?"

"That's what I want to discuss with you." replied the governor. "I'm not sure executing him would be to our advantage; politically speaking, that is."

While the two men discussed the fate of the condemned man, the sun was sinking behind a cloud that reached over the horizon.

The volcano belched forth more of its black smoke inland, thereby sparing St. Pierre more of its pumice fallout.

The sun had set and the day had become night very quickly because of the smoke from the volcano blowing onto that part of the island. When the pumice had finished falling, Father Mary left the church to go to Fort du France to report to the Vicar-General about the cultist's plans.

It was the intentions of both men that Andre should follow in half an hour so that in case Father Mary was caught by any cultists that might be lurking about, Andre could warn the Vicar-General in his stead.

When Andre finally left the church, the sky was reflecting the red glow of the lava boiling in the crater of Pelee. There weren't any flames shooting out of the volcano but at the same time the ground beneath his feet had a distinctive trembling effect.

Chapter Seventeen

Andre was able to see the road leading to St. Pierre and was on it for approximately twenty minutes when he noticed what appeared to be a small circular patch of deep red that was a hundred metres in width just below the summit of the volcano. At first, it was faint in colour, then it became cherry red and finally bright orange. Andre was confused at this unusual spectacle but as he trekked down the road, he suspected why the patch was there. For several days, one of the vents leading to the crater had gradually become blocked and the lava was now trying to escape through the side of the mountain.

Andre ran as fast as his legs could carry him for he suspected that the super heated gasses and lava would burst out of the side of the mountain like steam from a steam pipe. He estimated that from the angle that the circular plug was facing, he would need another kilometre of clearance if he was to be safe from the fiery death which would spew from that side of the mountain.

The ground began to shake violently and this spurred Andre to run even faster. Up ahead and in the distance, he saw a deserted hut just off of the road and he decided that he might be safer in the house than on the road. He judged that the initial blast would probably miss the area that he was in but that the immediate area of the hut would be sprayed with hot specks of lava cinders.

He ran into the hut and looked out of the window that faced Pelee. The circular path was facing him just off to his right. He stared at it, transfixed when suddenly the ground shook so violently that he was thrown off his feet. One of the walls of the hut crumbled to the ground. When Andre got to his feet, he looked back at Pelee. The circular patch began to disintegrate in the air. Behind the flaming patch, Andre could see the area left by the patch. It was like looking into a furnace. Hot lava shot out of the hole as Andre had predicted that it would. The spray of lava shot upwards for approximately a thousand metres and then arched over the countryside. The burning lava fell on the forests, cane fields and deserted hamlets. During this new onslaught, the noise was deafening and painful to his ears. Andre likened it to thousands of steamboats' whistles blowing. The brunt of the lava fell onto an area of approximately three kilometres long and one kilometre wide.

Fortunately, the hut Andre had chosen to seek shelter in was on the outskirts of the path of destruction. He could hear the pattering of small pieces of flaming lava falling about him and as he had expected, some had fallen on the roof of the hut.

In less than a minute, he could see the flames beginning to find their way through the rafters. He knew that he would have to leave the hut but the fear of being hit by burning embers kept him inside the hut despite the danger of a flaming roof.

Off in the distance to his right, about a half a kilometre down the road leading towards Morne Rouge, Andre could see the flames of the fires in the forest reaching high above the trees.

All about him pieces of lava were falling about the area, starting little fires in the grass. He decided he would have to escape from the area before the individual fires would turn into a huge inferno. He knew that if the fire got large enough, it would suck up the oxygen in the air and he would suffocate in the holocaust.

He bolted out of the hut and ran towards the road. He sidestepped the small smoldering fires that dotted the ground and when he reached the road, he ran as fast as his legs would permit. He didn't dare look behind him for fear that the burning embers might hit him square in the face or that the red hot dust blowing from Pelee might burn out his eyes. However as he ran, he watched in terror as small pieces of lava fell about him. He finally reached a bend in the road which was behind a hill that would protect him from direct contact with the specks of lava bombarding the area.

When he had got his breath back again, he continued to run towards St. Pierre and in less than half an hour he was on the outskirts of the city.

He looked behind him and watched with fascination at the display that Pelee was presenting to anyone looking at that direction. The fountain of lava was no longer there. The lava was now pouring out of the hole in the mountain and down the slopes. The whistling had ceased but a roaring sound could be heard coming from the area of Pelee. Flames shot high in the sky from the crater and disappeared into the clouds of smoke that hung over the volcano. Forks of lightning played around the summit, followed by peals of thunder.

Ciparis was looking out of the window in his cell, marveling at the volcanic display from Pelee when he heard footsteps approaching his door. He turned and saw four trustees enter his cell. One of the men locked the door behind him. He was then struck by one of the men and fell to the ground, only vaguely conscious of what was happening to him. As he sank to the floor and curled into a little ball, he brought up his knees close in order to protect his groin and with his arms about his head for protection. When the trustees were finished, they left him and one of the trustees before closing the door, spit at the whimpering form curled on the floor. Then the trustee snarled, "Listen, you son of a bitch! Just because the Governor has spared your life, doesn't mean that you are going to have a life of ease. You will pray for death every day for the rest of you life and curse the Governor for sparing your miserable life."

When the door slammed shut, Ciparis looked up at the ceiling and whispered, "God bless the Governor."

Andre reached Monique's house just as she was dressing to leave for work.

"Andre!" she exclaimed when she saw him at her doorway. "Where have you been? I thought that you would be here earlier."

"I am sorry, Monique. I got held up because of the lava flow from Pelee."

"Yes, I saw it. I really feared for you. I wasn't sure if you were trapped between Saint Pierre and Morne Rouge."

"I nearly was," replied Andre.

"Andre, there is something that I must tell you."

"Yes, I know. It's about your brother."

"You heard?"

"Yes, Father Mary told me," replied Andre. "Monique, I love you and I want to marry you and take you to France with me."

"I will marry you, Andre," said Monique as she embraced Andre.

Andre beamed as he hugged Monique and he knew he had made the right decision.

"Monique." He asked, "When is the earliest that you can be free to leave Saint Pierre?"

"When is the *Roraima* expected?" asked Monique.

"I understand it is expected on the morning of the eighth."

"Then tonight I will advise the owner of the club that tomorrow night will be my last performance."

"Good," replied Andre. "Then we will catch the *Roraima* on the eighth. As I understand it, the boat will be leaving in the afternoon so we had best be on it in the morning. Also, if the volcano erupts while we are on the boat, we have a better chance of surviving while in the harbour."

"What about Rene?" asked Monique in a disturbed tone, "He is planning to kill you."

"Fortunately, I know what he looks like so I will keep an eye open for him."

"Yes, but his followers will try to kill you too."

"Perhaps, but they don't know what I look like."

"I have an idea." said Monique. "As you know, I always wear a white flower in my hair when I dance in the cabaret. If I see Rene or his followers hanging about, I will put a red flower in my hair as a warning to you."

"That's a good idea," replied Andre.

"I have another idea that will keep Rene away from you, but you may not approve of it."

"What is it?"

"Perhaps if you waited for me in Fort du France for the next----."

Andre interjected, "No! Definitely not! I am this close to marrying you. I will not desert you at this difficult time in our lives."

"But Andre—."

Andre cut her short again, "Monique, I have an obligation to protect you for the rest of our lives. I won't run from it now."

"Very well, Andre," Monique replied in a subservient tone in her voice. "What ever you say is best."

The two walked out of her house, hand in hand and headed down the street. It was one o'clock in the morning when Monique had finished her dance routines at the club and she and Andre were on their way to her house. There had been no sight of Rene or his followers at the Cabaret and a glance at the volcano showed that there was nothing to fear from that quarter either. When they reached Monique's house, they glanced about to be sure that no one was lurking about in the shadows. Then when their privacy was assured, they entered her house. Andre wondered just how long they would be left alone, for it seemed that every night there was always trouble either from the mountain or Rene.

Half a kilometre away on the outskirts of the mulatto quarter, hundreds of men and women gathered in a square. The Voodoo wizards were chanting and urging their followers on.

Softly at first and then gradually louder, the drummers began to beat on their drums. The racklers and shuckers began to beat their sticks together. Torch after torch was lit until it appeared that every other person had a torch in his or her hands. The area lit up a bright yellow. The crowd became a column and soon they were moving towards the Rue du Collage. When they reached it they headed up the street that led into the city proper.

The Voodoo chant was like an intoxicating spirit that whipped up the crowd. Ahead of the column, the near naked dancers danced in such frenzy that their bodies glistened with sweat. Others from the column joined the dancers at the head of the column and began dancing their way up the street.

When they reached the Cathedral of St. Pierre at the end of Rue du Collage, the column became a large circle. Naked women were lifted into the air, their backs arched until their head and heels almost touched the ground. The tempo of the drumming increased and the dancers complied with the beat. Loud singing accompanied the fearsome sight.

Suddenly, a shot was fired into the air. The dancing, drums and singing stopped as if silenced by a sweep of one's hand. Into the center of the circle walked Rene Rousseau. Two of his followers trailed behind him, each carrying a chicken by its legs. The three Voodoo priests took their sacrificial victims to the cathedral door. The crowd was hushed as the three men took knives from their belts. In an instant, the throats of the goat and the chickens were slashed. The three men caught the blood in tin cups and when the cups were full, they drank the blood amidst a great sigh from the crowd. Then they hurled the dead animals against the cathedral door. Following the animals were the cups which clattered to the cobblestone street. The crowd turned to Rene who then screamed to his followers, "Let us go to the Mouillage Cemetery, for there we shall order all corpses which are whole to rise from their graves." The crowd ran down the street towards the cemetery, crying and chanting along the way. When they reached the cemetery, a group of cultists formed a large circle and within the circle, another group formed a small square. Within that group more cultists formed a cross. The drumming never varied its beat; low and consistent, it appeared to sustain the mood by its rhythm.

After a while, the drumming stopped and there was silence. The people carrying the candles and torches were darting all over the tombs. Then many of the candles were settled on one of the tombs. A suitable corpse had been found; one that had been interred just recently. Soon the stones were removed and hands clawed at the earth. The coffin was taken from the grave and hoisted high above the heads of the cultists. The cultists then moved out of the cemetery in single file with Rene and the coffin in the lead. The column moved into the darkness of the night until they looked like a winding snake with little flashing lights on its body. To anyone watching them, they saw the column winding itself up the hill behind the city and finally disappearing over the crest. Many of the townspeople were too terrified to follow for they knew that when the cultists get in this religious fever, it best to be at the opposite end of the city.

At three in the morning, molten lava swelled to the surface of the crater and began flowing down the slope. The bright orange of the lava lit up the sky, it reflection turned the gray ash on the streets of St. Pierre into a slight pink. Very few people were awake to notice the ever increasing brightness of the sky above Pelee or the subsequent outpouring of lava.

Fifty minutes later, everyone was awake. A thunderous explosion had rocked the city and the surrounding countryside. Thousands of tonnes of molten lava were ejected into the air. Pieces of the glowing rock, many weighing half a tonne or more, fell only a few hundred metres short of the town's boundaries. Pelee was entering another of its phases.

Andre and Monique were jolted out of bed. They rushed to the window facing the volcano. They were aghast at what they saw.

Another thunderous explosion rocked the city. At one moment a fiery outpouring of lava flowed over the surface of the volcano; at the next, long, perpendicular gashes of flame, pierced the column of smoke. Then a column of fire shot from them as if from a blast furnace.

There were four types of noises. First, the claps of thunder, which followed the lightning intervals of twenty seconds; then muffled detonations of the volcano like the roaring of many cannon fired in the distance simultaneously; third, the continuous rumbling of the volcano; and then the last, as though furnishing the base for this gloomy music, the deep noise of the suddenly swelling waters of all torrents which take their source upon the mountain, generated by an overflow such as had never yet been seen. This immense rising of thirty streams all at once caused flooding on the slopes because of the torrential rain falling on the slopes due to the tremendous condensation from the heat from the crater.

As everyone in the streets watched, a third tremendous loud explosion came from Pelee and again thousands of tonnes of white hot lava were ejected through the storm raging around the summit. The debris sailed through the air and fell on the already ruined village of Le Precheur and on the mud which had buried the Guerin factory. Red hot rocks fell into the sea, causing great splashes of water followed by great columns of steam in the air.

Panic was everywhere. The people ran down the streets again towards the sea, only to change their direction once again. Now they were running towards the southern part of the city. What they feared most was happening to them.

Like a creeping artillery barrage, the volcano was bombarding the northern edge of the mulatto quarter. As each minute passed, the rocks and pieces of lava fell upon the helpless victims, many of who were trying to escape through the streets. The houses caught fire when the burning rocks or lava plummeted through their roofs. Soon a dozen houses were blazing furiously.

The volcanic barrage ended almost as soon as it began but many of the houses were beyond any hope of saving. It appeared to many that the flames would not only engulf just the mulatto quarter but the entire city as well.

Through the panicked crowd came a troop of soldiers. The sight of them running towards the danger acted as a brake on the panic of the population. In their hands, they carried sticks of dynamite with blasting caps inserted in them and threw them into the blazing houses. The ensuring explosions; snuffed out the flames and destroyed the houses. They hoped that this would stop the fires from spreading.

By ten to five, Pelee's eruption had subsided momentarily but many of the town's people had had enough and were trekking out of the city in the direction of Fort du France. They were unable to reach their destination because Mayor Fouche had ordered all the roads leading out of the city be blocked. Soldiers turned the frightened townspeople back to St Pierre.

Andre and Monique were both dressed and discussing what they should do. "Monique, surely you must believe me when I say we must escape this city now?"

"I know there is reason to be alarmed Andre, but even if we left, we would have to return to the city docks to catch the *Roraima*."

"Yes, you're right on that point, Monique but the longer we stay out of Saint Pierre, the less chance we will be killed by the mountain. And there is your brother to fear also."

Just as Monique was going to make a reply, they heard a drumming noise in the distance. Both of them went to the door and looked out onto the street. Towards the southern end of the street, they could see a column of people carrying torches. They couldn't make out who or what they were, but as the column approached nearer to Monique's house, she felt a tingling sensation in her back. Then it dawned on her.

"Voodoo cultists." she said with a quivering voice.

"What?" asked Andre.

"It's the Voodoo cultists."

"You mean Rene's crowd?"

"Yes," replied Monique. "You must escape."

"You mean, we must escape!" said Andre with finality in his voice.

"No!" replied Monique. "Rene will not touch me. It's you he wants."

"But—"

"I will send them in the opposite direction."

Andre shifted uneasily and said, "I don't like this a bit."

The crowd came closer and soon Monique recognized her brother in the lead.

"You must leave now!" demanded Monique. Then her voice changed to one of pleading. "Please Andre. I will be safe but you must escape. Andre's leading them."

Just as Andre leaned towards Monique to kiss her, Monique yelled. "They have seen us! Quick inside! You can escape through the back!" Monique saw the crowd rushing up the street towards Monique's house. She wondered as she was locking the door if Rene would really kill her as Andre feared.

Andre was opening the window in the back of the house when he heard the banging on the door in the front of the house.

"Hurry!" yelled Monique. "Meet me at the club tonight and watch for the red flower in my hair."

Andre hesitated but as saw a torch passing one of the front windows, he opened the back window next to him and climbed out. As soon as his feet touched the ground, he ran as fast as he could. He looked behind him and saw the torches surrounding the house. He prayed for Monique's safety then bolted up the street.

Inside her house Monique, tried to hold the door closed, but just as she felt the door opening, hands pull her away from the door. A number of cultists had crawled through the window from which Andre had escaped. The door was forced open. In stomped Rene with a number of his followers.

"Where is he?" demanded Rene as he grabbed Monique's wrist.

"Of whom are you speaking of?" asked Monique.

Rene let go of her arm, then slapped her across the face. The impact knocked Monique to the floor."

"Get up and answer my question!"

"If you are speaking of Andre Verlaine, he's not here."

"I can see that! Where is he now?"

"I don't know," replied Monique.

"Do you want more?" asked Rene as he raised his arm.

"Turn her over to us!" yelled one of the cultists. "She will talk to us."

"Monique." said Rene in a voice that dripped in sweetness. "Surely you don't want me to turn you over to my men, do you?"

Monique knew that to continue denying any knowledge of Andre's whereabouts would be senseless because Rene would find out anyway so she decided to lie on the hope that Rene would accept anything over nothing at all. "He's gone to Fort du France."

"Why has he gone there?" asked Rene.

Monique answered, "Because he knows that I wont marry him and since he and Rachelle Hayot have broken up for good, he's decided to sail from Fort du France,"

"Why Fort du France?" asked Rene. "He could catch a boat from Saint Pierre."

Monique replied. "He's afraid of the volcano and believes that he will be safe in Fort du France."

"What boat is he going to catch?" asked Rene in a growling voice.

"I don't know." replied Monique.

Rene moved in close to his sister and in an instance, struck out at her with his fist. She fell to the ground. Then he demanded, "What boat?"

"Please, Rene. I really don't know."

Rene sneered. "If you are lying to me, I will return and kill you. Do you understand, sister?" She nodded affirmatively. She knew that he was the kind of man who would kill his own sister

Chapter Eighteen

Unbeknown to Monique, Andre had actually decided to go to Fort du France for the day and return later that night. He ran along the outskirts of St. Pierre and after fifteen minutes, he saw soldiers at the junction at Le Trace, the road leading to Fort du France. As he approached the soldiers, one of them called out,

"Where are you going?"

Andre replied, "Fort du France."

The soldier retorted, "Not today, you're not. The road is closed on orders of the Mayor."

"But I have to go there." continued Andre. "There are Voodoo cultists trying to kill me in St. Pierre."

The soldier yelled out again. "The road is closed!"

Andre knew that it was hopeless to argue with the soldier. He realized that the soldier was merely following orders. He turned and headed back to St. Pierre.

When he reached the center of the city, a group of men rounded the corner. He recognized one of the men. It was Rene.

Andre had walked right into the path of the cultists who were hunting him.

"After him!" screamed Rene as soon as he recognized Andre. Like one, the men turned towards Andre and charged after him. He knew that if they caught him, there would be no mercy from Rene and then he and his men would hack him to death with their machetes.

Andre began running for his life. As he ran up the street, his heart pounded and his lungs began to hurt terribly. He turned here and there and crisscrossed the city but to no avail. The cultists dogged his footsteps no matter how hard he tried to outpace them. He climbed over fences and ran through gardens and the cultists; forty all told, continued to chase him. At no time during his run did he see a soldier. He ran up the path leading to the hill behind the city, the same path Monique and he had earlier walked down, hand in hand. In the horizon, the morning sky was peeking out between the sea and the volcanic clouds.

Andre knew that the only place he would be safe would be at Morne Rouge for it was there that he knew that the villagers were unsympathetic to the causes of the cultists.

As he approached the spot where the road led into the forest, he saw a group of ten cultists approaching the two soldiers guarding the road. The soldiers, being wary of the approaching men, unslung their rifles and just as they were about to point them at the approaching men, the men lunged. In seconds, the soldiers were being throttled to death with wrapped cords of cured intestines of the cultist's former victims. Not one of them survived the cords; as the cords were light but had the tensile strength of cello strings. The two soldiers died before they had fallen to the ground.

Andre had been able to slip by the soldiers before they were attacked and when the soldiers had fallen to the ground, he bounded into the forest like a fleeting deer. After a few minutes of running through the forest, he decided to chance it by returning to the road. He couldn't take a chance of getting lost in the forest and further, the cultists would hear him crashing through the underbrush. If he wanted to slip away quietly, he knew that he would have to stay on the road.

After twenty minutes of continuous running, he arrived in the small village of Morne Rouge. He ran up to the church and banged on its front door. He screamed out, "Father Mary! Father Mary! Let me in! It's me, Andre Verlaine."

The cultists had been less than a minute behind Andre and while he was still banging on the church door, they spotted him. They ran towards him with even more determination to get him. Andre recognized Rene's voice when Rene called out. "You're a dead man, Verlaine."

His group had caught up to the other ten men who had killed the two soldiers and together they had entered the village. Now they were but ten metres away from their quarry. Just as Andre was about to take off again, he heard the bolt of the door being released. As the door began to swing open, the cultists were only five metres away from him.

"Quickly! Get in, my son." called out Father Mary as he pulled on Andre's arm.

Andre slid through the opening of the door. As he and Father Mary were closing it, Rene reached it and began pushing it open again. The two men behind the door managed to get it closed just as five of the cultists slammed their bodies against it. In a second, the bolt was secured with a loud click.

Andre sat down on the floor, gasping for breath. It was the first chance he had to get his breath back in over an hour.

"Thank God I got here in time." remarked Andre.

"What's made you choose our village?"

"I was being chased by the cultists. It seemed like the safest place to be at."

"Well, you sure picked a great place to run to." said the priest.

"Why?"

"Because this is just where the cultists intended to be this morning."

"What makes you say that?"

"I got word last night that they were planning to come here to kill me this morning. I thought the authorities in St. Pierre would have some soldiers standing guard at the road just outside of the city."

"There were," said Andre, "but the cultists killed them."

"I am sorry to hear that. It looks like we are on our own."

Suddenly there was a splintering of glass heard on one side of the church.

The priest shouted, "We will have to fight them at the windows."

"Have we anything we can use?" asked Andre as his eyes searched about.

"No, my son."

"Why, did you expect to be saved?" asked Andre.

"Yes I did. Perhaps we may be saved yet." Andre watched the priest go to the altar and kneel down before it and pray. Andre thought to himself, "*The priest can pray for both of us but as far as I am concerned, I will fight for both of us.*"

The cultists couldn't find any means to climb up to the high windows so they concentrated their efforts on the main door. They were attempting to batter it down and as the door began to give, Andre heard shouting from the distance. He ran to one of the windows and saw the coal women of the village running towards the church. In their hands were various farm implements and other tools.

"Father! Father! Come here!" yelled Andre. "Come here and look at this!"

The priest got up, crossed himself and ran down the aisle to the window where Andre was standing.

"Blessed be the Father." said the priest. "He has heard my prayers."

"You mean those women heard your prayers."

Those women that Andre spoke of descended upon the cultists. The cultists were no match for the fury of the coal women because of their sheer numbers and for this reason, the cultists began running away. The women chased them down the street into the arms of a group of hunters who had come to the village to protect the priest and his church. Shots were fired and a number of the cultists fell to the ground. They and some others who weren't shot and killed by the hunters were beaten to death by the coal women.

Andre could see that Rene was out of the range of the hunters' guns as he vanished into the forest surrounding the village.

Andre returned to the city in the early part of the afternoon and heard that the *Roraima* had arrived during the morning. He found the First Officer, Ellery Scott when he was at the booking office.

"Sir, I am Doctor Verlain."

"Yes Doctor. What can I do for you?"

"I am booking passage on your boat. When will you be leaving?"

"Tomorrow morning, about nine o'clock."

"There will be two of us, Sir."

Scott smiled and said, "From the looks of things, it appears there will be more than just two passengers leaving the city."

Andre looked about and saw the booking office crowded with evacuees planning to leave the city before the volcano exploded.

"Will it be possible to book a cabin?" asked Andre.

"Check with the booking clerk."

Andre did and was able to reserve a cabin for both himself and Monique. After he purchased the tickets, he then approached the First Officer again.

"When will your embarkation boats be taking us to the boat?"

"Tomorrow morning at seven thirty."

"Would it be possible to catch a boat just after midnight?"

"I don't think so, Doctor." replied Scott.

Andre told the First Officer about Rene and the cultists trying to kill him and that both he and Monique would be in great danger if they waited until dawn.

Scott gave his approval of Andre's request and said, "You can catch our cutter at three in the morning at the big pier with the rest of our crew."

Andre thanked the officer and then went to the cabaret where Monique would be rehearsing for her dance. She was just finishing one of her dances when Andre entered.

"Andre!" she exclaimed. "I'm so happy you're safe."

"I was worried about you too, Monique." said Andre as he embraced her. "Listen. I have some good news to tell you. I have arranged for us to catch one of the crew's landing boats tomorrow at three in the morning."

"Then I had better pack what things I will need for the voyage," replied Monique.

Together, the young couple left the cabaret and headed down the street towards Monique's house.

"Have you arranged with you boss to pay you?" asked Andre.

"Yes, as a matter of fact he has already paid me."

It was during the late afternoon that Andre decided to go to the park to sit in the sun so that Monique could rest before reporting to the Cabaret. While he was sitting on one of the benches he saw Rachelle walking through the park.

She spotted him and headed towards him.

Andre stood up and said, "Hello, Rachelle. It's good to see you again."

"Thank you Andre." replied Rachelle. "May I sit down with you?"

Andre nodded affirmatively and both sat down on the bench.

"I'm glad you didn't go to work the other day."

"All those children in the orphanage lost, because of the wave." said Rachelle partly to herself.

"It is most unfortunate, especially for you because you knew them all personally."

"How is Monique?" asked Rachelle.

"She is fine, thanks, Rachelle."

"Where did I go wrong with us, Andre?"

"I'm not blaming you, Rachelle," replied Andre. "You just weren't ready to assume the responsibilities of married life. You still want to dedicate your life to many rather than to one."

"Is that so wrong?"

"Of course not. Some people dedicate their entire lives to helping others and I have a great deal of admiration for them. But I am looking for a woman who will dedicate her life to me while I dedicate my life to many as a doctor."

Andre looked at Rachelle directly then replied, "I am returning to France tomorrow, Rachelle."

"Couldn't you wait until the end of the month? I will give you all the time and more."

Andre knew that when Rachelle spoke of giving more, she meant her body. He knew she was deeply sorry that their plans hadn't materialized. In his heart, he wished that they hadn't broken up.

After all, taking her to France was why he came to Martinique in the first place.

"Rachelle," began Andre. "I am taking Monique to France with me. We will be married tomorrow by the captain of the *Roraima*."

Rachelle looked away from Andre because she didn't want him to see the tears that began to flow from her eyes.

Andre sensed the emotional impact his remark had on Rachelle. Then he touched her face and she looked him in the face after wiping her eyes with the back of her hand.

"Rachelle, I hope that what I am going to say to you will make sense."

"What is that, Andre?"

"The solicited love clothed in silk is far exceeded by the unsolicited love clothed in rags."

"I understand its meaning Andre. I will never make that mistake again."

Andre replied, "I am sure of that, Rachelle. I do believe that someday you will make some man very happy when you marry him."

"Oh, thank you, Andre." said Rachelle as she embraced him. Then she left the bench and when she had walked several steps away, she turned and said, "I hope you will both be very happy. She is a good woman from what I have heard. Goodbye Andre."

"Goodbye Rachelle," Andre said as he waved his hand.

Rachelle turned and disappeared amongst the trees in the park.

It was just before midnight when Monique began her fourth dance of the evening. She had taken the precaution of looking for Rene and any of his followers that might be lurking around the floor. When she could plainly see that they were nowhere about, she placed her customary white rose in her hair and after fingering the red rose on her dressing table for a few moments, she left her dressing room to start her new dance. She had forgotten her red rose which she intended to hold in her hand while dancing and put in her hair if she spotted Rene.

She had been dancing for about two minutes when she suddenly spotted Rene as he entered the cabaret. He had some of his followers with him. It was clear to her that he was seeking Andre. She knew that with the white flower in her hair, Andre, if he came into the cabaret, would think that everything was safe. He would then go to Monique's dressing room when she had finished her dance and then would be followed by Rene and some of his men. Perhaps Andre wouldn't enter the cabaret until after the club was closed, or perhaps he would bring a police officer as an escort for the two of them. She had difficulty seeing across the enormous room because of the cigar smoke that created a bluish haze in the atmosphere of the room. It, as always, made her eyes smart.

Monique was about halfway through her dance when she first spotted Andre as he stepped through the door leading into the cabaret. He was alone. As she danced, her mind tried to find a way to warn Andre. She knew that without the red flower in her hair, Andre would be trapped into believing that everything was safe. Perhaps she could stop the dance and yell to Andre to escape. But she knew that wouldn't work either because Rene may have his followers go to the door to meet Andre on his way out. She thought, "If only there was a way to make the white rose into a red one."

Andre edged closer to center of the room so that he could catch sight of Monique dancing.

Monique could see Andre only occasionally because when she turned in her dance she would lose sight of him. Also, there were moments when she spotted Rene and at times both were almost next to each other without either of them being aware of the other's presence.

"A red rose," Monique whispered to herself. "How can I make a red rose out of a white rose?"

Then an idea struck her ravaged mind. She edged closer to a sailor who was sitting at a table. In an instant, she pulled the knife from the scabbard on his belt. The dumbfounded sailor made no effort to seize it because he assumed that it was going to be part of her dance.

Monique slowly drew the knife across her wrist. Blood spurted out over the blade and onto the floor. She then returned the knife to the sailor who was too confused to say anything in return. She took the flower out of her hair and while she danced to the rhythm of the drums in the small band, she dabbed the white rose into the open wound of her left wrist. Soon the rose had turned to a deep red colour. She placed the bleeding rose into her hair' some of her blood still dripping from the rose onto her face.

The members of the band were confused. They knew that Monique had mentioned that she might place a red rose in her hair but what she had done was not part of the act. The leader of the band felt that something was seriously wrong so he stepped up the tempo to end the dance. As the tempo increased, Monique danced even faster.

The crowd was completely aghast at what they were witnessing. They had never even heard of such an act, let alone see one like it before. The patrons clapped their hands to the music vigorously and cheered their favorite dancer on.

Monique whirled about the large room, her blood falling freely to the floor in little droplets.

"*If only Andre could get closer to see the red rose,*" she thought to herself. She attempted to edge closer to Andre when suddenly the music stopped. Monique knew that she would have to continue to dance until Andre spotted the red rose. As she kept dancing, many of the patrons kept clapping their hands to the tempo the band had been playing. The band leader realized that Monique was dancing for some reason other than just for show so he ordered the band to begin again and he increased the tempo because the patrons were keeping the original tempo with the clapping of their hands. Andre was moving about the crowd to find a place to sit and didn't see the red flower in Monique's hair.

Around and around Monique danced about the room, all the time becoming weaker by the minute.

"*God, please let Andre see the red flower in my hair.*" she cried to herself.

Her dance became more painfully noticeable to the patrons who cheered her on, as one of stumbling rather the usual graceful movements she made in the past. Still they couldn't comprehend what made her do what she was doing because they were hypnotized by what they were seeing.

"He's seen the flower!" thought Monique as she saw Andre run out of the cabaret into the street. *"Thank God."* she said faintly to herself.

She decided she would dance her number through and finally amidst the cheering and clapping of the patrons she finished her dance. She stumbled into her dressing room and fell unconscious onto the floor in a heap.

Andre meanwhile ran to the police station for help. He finally convinced the police of the necessity of escorting both of them from the cabaret to the police station and finally to the big pier. When they arrived at the cabaret, they had difficulty in getting through the crowd. When they did, they entered Monique's room and found her lying on her back with a piece of cloth wrapped around her wrist.

"Monique! Monique!" cried Andre as he knelt down to her. "What happened?"

"She cut her wrist with a sailor's knife during her dance." answered one of patrons standing in the room.

"Why Monique?" asked Andre. "I promised you that we would be married."

Monique opened her eyes and looked into Andre's face. "It was the flower, Andre."

Andre looked at the flower and saw the blood still in it. When he realized the truth, he lifted Monique's head into his arms and kissed her and asked. "Why didn't you wear the red flower?"

"I forgot and left it in my dressing room. You were not in the cabaret when I began my dance." Then Monique gave him a small smile and said in a feeble voice. "I'm sorry, Andre. I don't think that I will be able to go to France with you tomorrow."

Andre stroked her hair and replied, "That's alright, Monique. I will wait around until you get better and we will go at a later date."

Monique grasped Andre's hand and whispered, "I mean—that it's—too late."

"No!" sobbed Andre as he began hugging her. "It's not too late. The doctor's coming." He looked at the crowd and then asked them, "Isn't he?"

A voice replied from the crowd. "The doctor has been sent for."

"See." said Andre. You will be alright, you'll see."

Monique was fading fast and she wanted to say what was to be said to Andre before it was too late. She whispered, "Andre—I talked with Rachelle. She loves you—she told me—Promise me that if I die, you will not forsake your love for her. Promise me—please."

Andre began, "But—."

"Promise me—."

I promise." replied Andre as he hugged her even tighter.

"Remember Andre, that I—that I—."

Andre stared into Monique's eyes and asked, "What do you want me to remember, Monique?"

He knew that Monique couldn't answer him. He sensed it when he felt the slight shudder in her body. He knew it when he realized that her eyes were now staring beyond his own and into the face of God.

The room was completely hushed. Not a person moved nor spoke. Andre gently lowered Monique's head onto the floor again. A voice within the crowd whispered, "White Flower was the greatest dancer of them all. What more needs to be said about her?"

Andre knew of course that a great deal more could be said about her. But he would keep that to himself. It was better, he felt, that those who knew her, remembered her as the greatest dancer of them all. She was the 'Great White Flower' of the islands. They would talk about her final dance for generations to follow; if not forever.

Andre stood up and faced the patrons. As the tears ran down his face, he cried out for all to hear. "White Flower has proved to us that if self-preservation is the first law of nature, then self-sacrifice is the highest rule of grace."

A voice cried out, "Amen." Others repeated the response.

Chapter Nineteen

Andre stood up and looked down at the bleeding form at his feet. The patrons noticed the sadness in his face vanish and anger take its place. If Rene Rousseau wanted him how, he wouldn't have to search for him. He would find Rene instead. He knew where Rene would be. He would have gone to Monique's house. Andre bolted out of the room screaming, "Rene, you bastard! Here I am! Wait for me! I am coming for you!"

As he passed one of the policemen, he grabbed his pistol. Before the policeman had a chance to stop Andre, he began running down the street.

Andre was about halfway to Monique's house when he became aware that it was still raining outside. Flashes of lightning lit up the darkened streets. Loud crashes of thunder followed almost instantly. He realized that the storm was directly over the city as well as the volcano.

He saw Monique's house up ahead during a flash of lightning. It was during the next flash, when he was about six metres from it, that he saw a figure at the open door. It was Rene.

Andre aimed the pistol and fired. Rene clutched his arm, and then ran around the side of the house.

Andre followed but when he got there, Rene was gone. He listened and could faintly hear the sound of feet crashing through the underbrush. A flash of lightning pointed out Rene in the neighbour's yard climbing over a fence.

"Come back!" screamed Andre.

Rene made no reply but continued to run in the direction of the volcano.

"You can't escape me, Rene. There is no one to save you now."

Rene reached a street and began running up it. Andre followed behind him by twenty metres. He could barely make out Rene's image when the lightning flashed. The street was completely deserted. The rain came down in a deluge. It almost made it impossible to see Rene during those flashes of lightning. The chase took them up and down streets, along the waterfront, behind houses, in the park and through the square.

It was while running up the Rue Victor Hugo, St. Pierre's main street that Andre saw a bolt of lightning hit someone up ahead.

He ran to the stricken figure but couldn't make out who it was. It was too dark. He would have to wait till a flash of lightning would appear again and light up the scene. He didn't have to wait long. It wasn't Rene, but another victim of Pelee.

Andre ran up the street praying that Rene didn't turn up one of the streets that cut across Victor Hugo. He listened for sounds of Rene but instead heard a distant roaring sound. It wasn't Pelee. It was the Roxelane River. The storm had caused the river to overflow its banks and was dragging debris from the edge of its banks. Boulders, trees, animals and humans were being swept down the river from the hinterland. By the time the river had reached the centre of the city, the river was a seething cauldron of swirling water and debris.

Andre knew that if Rene had run towards the river he would have to turn back for there was no longer any bridge to cross. The city was completely bisected. He saw Rene up ahead in one of the flashes of lightning. He was standing on a ledge that jutted over the river. It was during the next flash that Rene saw his mentor.

"Don't kill me. Please," cried Rene.

"You intended to kill all of us." replied Andre. "Why should I let you live now?"

"Because you are a doctor. You save lives?"

"I would give up my vocation permanently just for the opportunity to kill you."

The flashes of lightning were becoming more frequent; one every ten seconds.

Andre continued, "You killed Monique, and for that, you are going to die."

"I loved my sister. I wouldn't kill her. She killed herself."

"She died trying to save me from you and your henchmen," said Andre angrily.

"You can't kill me for that."

"I can and I will." answered Andre. "You are a pig. You shouldn't be allowed to live. There is no place for you in our world."

"Then if you kill me, you will be no different than I am. At least I kill for a purpose. You are killing with vengeance as your only motive."

Andre sneered at his victim. "You planned the wholesale murder of innocent people knowing that by doing so, it would benefit your own needs. Your motives are no less honourable than mine."

"How can you judge me? You are only a visitor to this island."

"I am not judging you as a resident of this island but rather as a man with a conscious. If I let you live, you will continue to kill for your own needs."

Andre cocked the revolver and aimed it at Rene. He could just make out his figure. Rene sensing that in an instant, he would be shot, lunged towards Andre.

Andre squeezed the trigger and felt the gun kick in his hand. His ears hurt from the sound of the report.

Rene stopped short as if punched in the stomach, his mouth opened, as if gasping for air.

"Now turn around and jump in the river where your body will be swept out to sea away from the land you would defile with your presence," yelled Andre.

"Damn you," sobbed Rene as he clutched at his belly. "Damn you!"

Andre squeezed off another shot and Rene's right hand reached for his left shoulder. He stumbled slowly towards his executioner.

Again Andre fired another shot and Rene reached instinctively up to his right shoulder where the bullet smashed into his collarbone.

"Please, no more." pleaded Rene.

"Then take your chances in that watery coffin that awaits you." Andre demanded.

"No, I can't" replied Rene.

A flash of lightning lit up the macabre scene and Andre squeezed off another shot. The bullet entered Rene's left leg, just above the knee. Rene dropped to his knees.

"Now crawl to your coffin like the pig you are." Andre yelled.

Rene realized that the next bullet would be in his head so he turned and crawled over the ledge and dropped into the river. In an instant, he vanished beneath the raging water.

Seconds later, Andre saw Rene's hand reach out of the water in desperation. With all the strength that he could muster, Andre threw the pistol after Rene. Then he turned away from the river and suddenly his stomach felt queasy. He vomited until he was sure his stomach was going to be torn apart. Never before had he killed anyone or seen a man die like that. He prayed that he would never do or see another such killing.

Andre slowly walked back to Monique's house. He planned to spend the night there and catch the landing boat in the morning as originally planned.

When he arrived at Monique's house, there was a small crowd just outside her door. Inside, a number of her close friends had placed Monique's body on her bed. They left knowing Andre wanted to spend some time with Monique. Andre knelt down beside her body and wept. After he was in the house for an hour, he heard a slight noise behind him.

"Andre," whispered the voice from behind him.

He turned and could just make out the image from the feeble light of the candle. He knew from the voice that it was Rachelle.

"Hello Rachelle," replied Andre as he wiped his eyes. "What brings you here?"

"I heard about Monique. I came to see if there was anything I could do."

"Thank you, Rachelle," said Andre. "I would be grateful if you could see to Monique when I leave."

"I already have," answered Rachelle.

"You have?"

"Yes, I spoke to Father Mary. He said that he would look after everything."

"How could—?"

Rachelle interjected, "He has been in St. Pierre all night."

Andre led Rachelle to the room at the front of the house. "Thanks for being concerned, Rachelle."

"It was the least that I could do," replied Rachelle then she added, "Poor Andre. You have traveled so far and have lost the one you really loved."

"You know, Rachelle, the person I really came to marry was you, but fate being what it is, it caused me to fall in love with Monique instead."

"You fell in love with the better of the two of us," said Rachelle. "But I have learned a valuable but bitter lesson."

"What's that?"

"I really love you, Andre, but my mistake was that I didn't show it. Love must not only be so, it must appear to be so."

"Somehow I had the feeling that you weren't prepared to give up your inheritance and return to Paris with me."

"Andre, I would have given up everything to marry a man such as you—even my family, friends and the plantation."

"That is giving up a great deal, Rachelle."

Rachelle thought for a few seconds then replied, "Perhaps, but Monique gave her life for you. Giving up all my friends, family and so forth is nothing compared to Monique's sacrifice. Knowing of her sacrifice would only make my actions bearable. Monique would be alive if I had sacrificed my ambitions in Martinique instead."

Andre realized that Rachelle was probably suffering feelings of guilt. He knew that Rachelle was probably blaming herself for Monique's death.

"You don't have to shoulder the blame yourself, Rachelle. If I hadn't fallen in love with Monique, she would be asleep in her bed instead of dead in her bed."

"Andre, do you think there could be a chance for us again?"

Andre thought the question over in his mind then replied, "It would mean leaving Saint Pierre right away before you could get your parent's consent."

"I have their consent." replied Rachelle. "I told them that I was going to try and win your love again. They told me that they would pray for my success."

"You mean your mother approves of me finally?"

"She always approved of you, Andre. It's just the prospect of me leaving the island that was hard for her to face." Then Rachelle laughed and said, "And of course Father always said that you were the best catch on this island."

"He said that?"

"Yes, and he said that and while I was trying to prepare the bait for you, Monique was reeling you in. He said that that was the difference between myself and Monique. We both wanted you but she knew how to get you, I didn't."

"Do you still want me?" asked Andre.

"Yes, with all my life."

"Please, I don't want you giving your life for me as Monique did." I want to dedicate my life to you, Andre. All of it."

Andre embraced Rachelle. He knew that she was the same girl he met in Paris. He wouldn't try to compare her with Monique but he knew he could be happy with Rachelle.

"We owe our happiness to Monique," said Rachelle.

"And my life," added Andre.

"Yes, of course. Incidentally, what became of her brother Rene?"

"He will bother no one anymore," replied Andre.

Rachelle suspected that Andre probably killed him but she knew that if he did, he was justified.

Outside, the air was becoming a bit warmer. Andre turned to Rachelle and asked, "Would you like to return to Paris with me as my wife? We can be married by the captain."

"Oh yes!" answered Rachelle.

"Then we had better go to the waterfront and wait for the landing boat. Just wait a minute outside." said Andre as he went back to Monique's room. He went to her bed and leaned over and kissed Monique on her lips and whispered, "Goodbye Monique. I shall never forget you."

Andre stepped out of the house and after closing the door, he and Rachelle walked down the street hand in hand towards the waterfront. The sky in the east was a deep purple. They knew the colour was from the sun behind the mountain trying to shine through the dust in the air.

Chapter Twenty

Meanwhile, the volcano had been quiet. The people of St. Pierre began to believe that Pelee would go to sleep at last. What they didn't know was that several kilometers below the surface of the earth, immense pressures were building up. The lava, its temperature having reached thousands of degrees, was becoming white hot. When the volcano couldn't hold back the pressure any longer, it roared back to life. First the ground shook followed by a low rumbling noise followed. As each brief moment passed, the sound of the rumbling increased until the noise was deafening. Andre and Rachelle instinctively clasped their hands to their ears.

Explosions occurred at intervals of from five to ten minutes, each of these outbursts uncovering the liquid lava in the vent, the glow of which lighted up the overhanging steam-cloud for a few seconds.

They watched the flames shoot out of the crater, followed by white smoke which reflected tints of red from the flames. Shortly the smoke changed to brown with the flames intertwined inside it. The smoke belched upwards thousands of metres as if never to return to earth.

By half past five, the sun had risen over the horizon and the sky in the east had changed from purple to bright pink. By the time the young couple had reached the centre of the city, hundreds of people had gathered at the cathedral even though Mass wouldn't be heard until 7:30 in the morning.

In the streets, the panic had subsided because news of the Governor being in the city had circulated. After all, if he would venture into St. Pierre, then it probably meant that there wasn't any real danger expected from Pelee. There were many people standing outside the doors of the Hotel de L'Independence where the Governor and his wife were staying while in the city. Soon, he would emerge and probably make a speech about Pelee re-telling everyone that everything was safe.

Father Roche had climbed Mount Verde to get a better look at the raging volcano. By six o'clock the smoke had changed to red with the fringes being brown and black. The smoke had blown inland and blotted out the rising sun and the earlier pink sky. The city and surrounding countryside as well as the harbour were in complete darkness accept for the lanterns that occasionally lit up small patches of the area in the city.

Just after six o'clock, a tremendous explosion rocked the area. Father Roche's eyes became transfixed on the summit of Pelee. Enormous rocks were projected out of the crater. Many of them, more than a tonne in weight, arched so high over the countryside, that it took as long as fifteen seconds before they finally crashed into the forests below. More detonations from the crater brought more of the enormous rocks out of the crater of the raging volcano. Father Roche knew that there were probably a number of submarine craters inside Pelee from which gasses were being forced out. Every two or three seconds, large sheets of flames burst from the centre when the gasses made contact with the air outside. Much of the flames were white hot. The heat from Pelee could be felt all the way to Mt. Verde. The air became suffocating and the priest found himself shielding his face from the burning heat.

Ciparis was jarred from his sleep when Pelee first blasted the large rocks out of its crater. He went to his window to look out but found that much of the ash that had earlier swirled about in the yard was now piled up against the northern walls of the building in the prison, like sand drifts. He could just barely see out of a small opening of 5 centimeters high and approximately 15 centimeters in length. All he could see were flashes of red and orange lighting up the low handing clouds over the city. Other than that, it was pitch black outside. Often he wished that his cell had faced Pelee so that at least he could pass the time away by watching the volcano perform its antics.

Soon he became aware of the dust blowing through the small opening of the window. He knew that the smoke had drifted down on the city again. In order to reduce the amount of choking dust blowing in, he tried blocking the opening of the grill with his shirt but it kept blowing back into his cell. He urinated on his shirt and wrapped it around his head then curled up in a corner of his cell, clasping his arms around his knees. The air in the cell became warmer by the minute. Within minutes the grill was completely blocked with ash so that no more dust was swirling about in his cell. He pulled the shirt away from his head and stared into the blackness of his cell. It was still hot and stuffy in his cell and the perspiration poured from his body. But at least he could breathe a little easier.

The first mate of the *Roraima* was on deck by the time the first detonation was heard and for the next hour and a half, he watched the volcano. Captain Muggah had also been awakened by the initial blast, but he had his hands full with the company agents from St. Pierre. They wanted the *Roraima* to remain in the harbour for the rest of the day as they had arranged for the extra barrels of rum to be shipped out on the *Roraima*.

The rum had been placed along the wharves of the waterfront and there was a good commission for all if they could be shipped out. The captain wanted no part of this. He wanted to leave the harbour as soon as possible. There were a number of his crew to return with the last landing boat, then the *Roraima* would steam from the island as fast as it engines would propel it.

Meanwhile a number of sailors were cleaning up the ash which had settled on the decks of the boat. Many of the twenty-one passengers and forty-seven crew members were saving some of the ash as little mementoes of the occasion.

At twenty minutes to eight, the dust and smoke had blown inland and the sun began to shine through the dust laden air as a hazy spot of light. Within a few minutes the sun was shining brightly and the volcano quieted down. To Ellery Scott, the first mate, everything now appeared favourable and pleasant. Pelee was calm except for a circular red glow in the rocks just below the summit.

Fernand Clerc could hear the bells of the Cathedral ringing to summons the faithful to church. Even though it was Ascension Day, he had the distinct feeling that there were more faithful in the city today than ever before. Nature always had its way of making true believers out of sinners. He looked down on the city from his balcony. He was always glad he had chosen the hill behind the city to build his house on. From his house he got a magnificent view of the city and the harbour. He watched from a distance, the crowd of people outside the cathedral. These were the people who would have to attend the church services outside, as the church had been filled hours before.

He could hear his children laughing in the carriage at the entrance of his house. Ever since the first volcanic detonations at six, he had decided that it would be safer for him to have his family inside the carriage so that if the volcano erupted, they could move out instantly.

He stared at the volcano and noticed that there was a red patch just below the summit. He estimated that it was several hundred metres below the summit. What concerned him the most was that the circular patch was facing the city. He remembered the same type of patch exploding a couple of nights previously. Fortunately the blast of lava had burned an area east of the city. He knew the end of the city was near. He realized that even though the volcano was six kilometers from St. Pierre, the blast area of the circular patch would reach as far as the city. He prayed that the people in the city would realize it also. He looked at his barometer and watched the needle swing from side to side. The time had come. He ran downstairs and leaped into the carriage. Soon he and his family were headed away from their plantation. Their destination was a hill a kilometre away to the west.

Andre and Rachelle had reached the waterfront earlier at seven-fifteen. The waterfront had been crowded because many of the people weren't sure of the fate that Pelee had in store for them. What ever it was, the safest place would be the waterfront where they could jump into the water.

Andre was able to finally convince the shipping authorities at the main wharf that although Monique had been listed as the other passenger, Rachelle was the actual passenger who would be taking Monique's place. As it was, the authorities were being very careful who was leaving the city as the Pox was still prevalent. When the officer of the landing boat was sure that Rachelle and Andre didn't have the Pox, he let them into the boat. It wasn't until eight-thirty that the landing boat pulled away from the wharf with its boatload of passengers and crew.

When the oarsmen had rowed the boat several hundred metres into the harbour, it was then that Andre saw the red circular patch glowing just below the summit. When he saw the direction of the expected blast-area, his heart began to beat until he thought it would burst. He tried to gasp out what was on his mind but he choked on the words. Finally he got the words out. "Get this boat out of here fast! The volcano is going to explode!"

"Explode?" asked the officer in charge.

"Yes." replied Andre. "The other night, the same type of circular patch exploded, just to the right of the volcano and burned an area for many kilometres."

The crew, on hearing Andre's remarks, began pulling on their oars as hard as they could. Fear began to show itself on the faces of the crew and passengers alike. The *Roraima* was still a hundred metres away.

On Mt. Verde, Father Roche looked with horror at the circular patch facing St. Pierre. He knew that within minutes, the inside of the volcano would reach its critical point and thousands of tonnes of red hot rocks would be sent hurtling onto the town six kilometres away. He knew that if that happened, the city and everyone in it, would be doomed.

Suddenly, an ear-shattering loud bang like the sound of a cannon fired up close was heard from the area of Mt. Pelee.

The explosive eruption ejected a dark-grey ash-laden vertical cloud into a column of ash that would reach upwards of eleven kilometres above the summit. The bulk of the ejecta was moving at the rate of 200 kilometres an hour skyward for the first moments after the eruption's onset.

As the pulses of the dense ash rose above the summit, blocks of rock were ejected high into the sky before falling to earth and crashing through the forests at the base of the mountain. The enormous extrusion of viscous, silica-rich lava erupted at the surface and into the atmosphere as mixtures of red-hot pumice, volcanic ash. (small, jagged fragments of volcanic glass and rock) The ash cloud formed by smaller avalanches was diffuse enough so that boulders below the summit could be at first seen rolling slowly down slope. Blue flames were observed in the vents near the summit, at times flickering and jumping from one vent to another. An anvil-shaped steam and ash cloud grew, producing ash that would fall as far away as Fort de France, leaving a thin layer of light grey-colored, abrasive material on the ground. Meanwhile, numerous lava flows descended the flanks of Pelee at the beginning of the eruption, reaching the timberline in seconds.

Within ten seconds of the initial blast, and at a spot further down from the base of the column of ash that was rising above the summit and what was on the southwestern side of the volcano, (the one Andre was staring at) a powerful laterally-directed blast of superheated gray ash and poisonous sulfur-dioxide gas blew outward with enormous force from an area on that side of the mountain facing St. Pierre and in less than a second, it overtook the avalanche of rocks that had preceded it. The superheated ash avalanche began flowing down its flanks at a speed of three hundred kilometres an hour. The boulders ahead of it seemed to be only partially fluidized by the superheated ash and traveled no more than several hundred metres beyond the base of the talus below the cliffs. The ash cloud meanwhile rolled over the avalanche and moved down slope at the same speed as before.

The onslaught of incandescent super-heated ash with a temperature of over 800 degrees Centigrade, rushed towards the base at the southwestern side of the mountain devastating the area as it rolled across the forests. The powerful lateral blast blew over all of the trees near the volcano, leaving jagged stumps with splinters facing away from the volcano parallel to the direction of movement of the blast cloud. The leaves and barks were burned off, leaving bare blackened logs on the ground.

The pyroclastic cloud of death continued on towards the city as it crossed over the fields and then down the narrow valley towards the city as if it was targeted in the sights of a rifle. It struck the city with the impact of an enormous tidal wave as it rolled over and through the city and then extended itself across the harbor. In less than half a minute, the pumiceous pyroclastic flow had traveled six and a half kilometres from the crater of the volcano, through the forest and the fields, through the city, across the harbor and over the surface of the immediate sea before it was eventually dissipated in the wind. The pyroclastic flow, generated both by the collapse of the vertical column in the volcano and the direct emission through the large southward breach produced by the directed blast, left a fan-shaped pumiceous deposit extending several kilometres from the mountain overlying the previous debris flow deposits in that area.

On Mount Verde, Father Roche had felt a gust of hot wind strike his face. When he opened his eyes again, he saw many trees being blown to the ground, their branches being stripped of their ash-laden leaves. Even some of the smaller braches were being broken off. The hot wind had gusted down the slopes of Pelee and crossed the valley and continued on its journey up Mount Verde. When the wind had passed, Father Roche noticed the vapors from the summit chasing each other as they were swept upwards by tornado-like air currents. The priest began crying for the doomed city and its inhabitants. He knew that it was only a matter of seconds before the overheated ash would kill all of the thirty thousand people in St. Pierre. The similar explosion of several nights previous had shown him what Pelee would do to everyone caught in its path.

When Andre was originally staring at the mountain, his eyes had previously perceived the growing bright orange ball of fire which had grown out of the area where the red patch had been. For a brief moment it hung there on the upper slopes of the volcano. The sound of the explosion reached his ears and he and the others instinctively clasped their hands to their ears to protect their eardrums from the awesome blast. Andre noticed the time on his watch as he raised his hand. It was seven-forty-nine. The roar of the eruption now sounded to him like a thousand cannons being fired all at once. When he drew his hands away from his ears, he could hear the initial sharp blast echoing between Pelee and Verde. He could see that the circular patch of red-hot rock had detached itself from the side of the volcano. He watched with fascination as the fire with the black clouds of smoke swirling from it began rolling down the slopes of the volcano towards the city like a giant black boiling tidal wave. The noise accompanying the wave was a continuous muffled roar with intermittent blasts, like the staccato beats of a machine gun.

At about the same time, another loud explosion occurred and an enormous Vulcanian cloud of thick black ash shot out of the crater and headed straight into the sky above. When the cloud had reached a height of seventeen kilometres above the summit of the volcano, it began to spread out in all directions, towards the horizons surrounding the island from all sides.

Black smoke continued to pour out of the gaping hole in the volcano where the ball of fire had emerged. The smoke followed behind the fireball and then it rose straight up into the sky to join with the Vulcanian column of ash. The forests burst into flame as the pyroclastic fireball inside the black smoke separated itself from the column of ash above it emanating from the crater and the searing hot pyroclastic ash began proceeding down the mountain engulfing everything in its path. The smoke emitting from the crater spread across the sky and blotted out the sun until the entire countryside was in complete darkness. All that could be seen was a sliver of light in the horizon behind him.

Andre could see flames that were submerged in the smoke, poking their way out of the black smoke only to disappear in more of the volcanic dust. No one could understand why the flames were hugging the ground rather than shooting upwards as the wave of fire headed towards them at a hundred metres a second. What was happening during these frightful moments was something never seen by anyone on the island before. It was a *nuee ardente* or glowing cloud, the most fearsome of all volcanic eruptions—a horror than no one can possibly survive in. The wave of death poured down the large V-shaped notch that centuries before had cut through cliffs surrounding the summit crater. Andre stared at the sight in absolute terror. He recognized that most of the damage in Pillean eruptions, such as Pelee comes not from lava flow but from a phenomenon known as a pyroclastic flow. The pyroclastic flow coming from the side of Pelee was a ground-hugging hot cinders and super heated ash accompanied by poisonous gas racing down the slope of the volcano at a high speed.

The glowing avalanche of minute super-heated incandescent rock fragments continued flowing down the valley of the Blanche River not unlike like an avalanche of snow. The glowing avalanche kept to the bottom of the valley which at this point on the mountain, was headed straight for the city. But when the *nuee ardente* reached a bend in what was now a canyon in which the Blanche River flowed, the wave of fire and ash jumped the ridge on the south side of the canyon and continued moving southward towards the doomed city just less than a kilometre below it. The length of the awesome monster was just over one kilometre and was now spreading outwards until it was two kilometres in width with the cloud of fire over sixty metres in height.

Shooting through the surface of the red billowy avalanche were large pyroclastic stones which stood out as streaks of bright red. They tumbled down the mountain emitting showers of sparks as the pyroclastic lava material, with its soft molten lava inside, exploded upon impact with the harder surfaces of the ground. Fernand Clerc called to his family which he knew was near him even though he couldn't see them because of the sudden darkness enveloping them. He could hear his children crying out in fear. Even though they were on Mount Parnasse, twelve kilometres from Pelee, there were doubts in his mind as to whether they would be safe from what he expected to come from Pelee.

A hurricane-like wind, acting as the forerunner of the fiery monster that had reached them, almost blew them off their feet. Clerc watched the fearsome glowing fireball which to him seemed as if it was well over half a kilometre in diameter, approach the northern extremities of St. Pierre.

The sea breezes gently blowing in from the harbour began rushing towards the wall of death approaching it to feed the monster cloud with the oxygen it needed. The buildings in the northern part of the city were the first to crumble from the shock of the blast, trapping its inhabitants so that they couldn't escape from the fearsome onrushing glowing ash that would burn their bodies to a crisp; not that escaping was an option. Within seconds, the wall of death was only a block away from the centre of the city. Those in the immediate area of the onrushing wall of death, felt the air being sucked out of their lungs. They began gasping for air that was no longer there. They became unconscious from suffocation even before the super heated ash reached their bodies. Within seconds, all traces of life in St. Pierre was extinct. The entire population of thirty thousand residents and visitors in the city had suffocated to death and now their bodies were being incinerated by the super heated ash. It mattered not whether the victims were inside their homes or other buildings. There is no escaping death when they were enveloped by the pyroclastic flow of super heated gas which in itself, was also poisonous. Many of the worshippers in the cathedral had previously poured out of the church in an effort to escape what was to become their inevitable death, while others remained behind to pray.

The governor while standing next to the window of the hotel he was in, had marveled at the way great streaks of lightning flashed through the black smoke right after the initial explosion had brought him and his wife to the window of their room. The flames reached high in the sky until they seemed to go deep into the heavens. He watched with his wife beside him as the tornadic suction of the air, being drawn into the fire, dragged screaming men, women, children, animals, trees and other loose debris along the streets towards the flaming inferno inside the black ash that was approaching them. They left the area of the window when they saw the black cloud heading towards the center of the town. Within seconds, their entire room was in total darkness. The window blew outwards to meet the roaring flames. In an instant, everything in the room burst into flames and was incinerated.

Meanwhile, Ciparis could faintly hear the screaming down the corridor of the prison but couldn't see anything because his cell was in complete darkness. Then he felt dirt falling on his face. The ground shook violently. He could hear the sound of stone blocks crumbling to the ground. He felt that the end of his life had arrived. He prayed to his God as the walls of the building he was entombed in came tumbling down around his ears. The powerful wave of air accompanied by an earthquake had caused all the other stone buildings in the city to also crumble.

The landing boat arrived at the *Roraima* just as the burning cloud passed over the entire city. The fireball smashed into the hill a kilometre from the southern part of the city and rose straight up into the air. A good part of the fireball bounced back onto the city to sweep over the city's streets and buildings with its deadly fire to continue incinerating the inhabitants in the crumbled buildings who by then were already dead.

Some of the black wave of death headed into the harbour. Andre watched as the *Grappler*, one of the boats in the harbour, turned over on its side and slip under the water as the wave of super-heated ash hit it broadside. The deadly black wave continued on towards the other boats in the harbour. The sailing boats immediately caught fire and those that weren't perpendicular to the fireball turned onto their sides and sunk whereas those that were perpendicular to the wave caught remained upright in the water but caught fire and within minutes, were blazing infernos.

Andre and Rachelle scrambled aboard and ran towards an open hatchway. He pushed Rachelle through the hatchway and after running a few steps down a passageway ahead of her; he stopped at an open door and pulled Rachelle into the cabin. He ran to the porthole and slammed it closed just as the super-heated fire and ash reached the boat.

The blast hit the *Roraima* and rolled it far to port, then with a sudden jerk, she rolled to starboard, plunging her guardrails under the surface of the water. Then the boat righted itself. The blast had swept the masts and smokestack clean off of the deck and many of the passengers who hadn't escaped in time and were being burned alive, were swept into the sea where a merciful death by drowning awaited them.

Inside the cabin, Andre and Rachelle had been thrown off balance at the first impact and fell to the deck. The cabin suddenly became hot as if they were too close to a bonfire. The cabin was lit up a bright orange as the fireball passed over the boat, the light penetrating their closed eyelids.

Chapter Twenty-one

Outside their cabin, Andre and Rachelle could hear the agonizing screams of the victims as they were being burned alive. When the burning cloud hit them, the red hot dust particles were inhaled by the people still on the deck as they screamed, which then resulted in their lungs being burned to a crisp. Suffocation came instantly for some of them. But for the others, it was far worse. Those whose lungs hadn't been burned, were now choking to death as their throats, seared by the intense heat, were almost entirely closed.

The entire boat was aflame from one end to another and the anchor was dragged deeper into the mud at the bottom because of the onrush of the force of the hot wind that hit the boat. The boat was stuck fast to await further torments from Pelee.

At the immediate outskirts of St. Pierre, every man, woman and child was a burning torch. Many were blinded by the intense heat or by the searing red hot specks of dust that burned their eyes out of their sockets. Children screamed, their tongues burned out of their mouths. The hair of the inhabitants flared up in a bluish flash in an instant, then the skin of their scalps began to peel. Many of the people who had the foresight to close their eyes as the death cloud struck, could see when they finally opened them. What they saw caused many to pass out, never to regain consciousness; their flesh had been dropping off their bodies like melted wax.

The thousands of barrels of rum and sugar that were on the wharves and side streets had exploded. The flaming contents poured down the streets and into the water. The entire waterfront was an inferno. All those who jumped into the water to save themselves were doomed by the flames on the surface of the water. No matter how many times they submerged under the water to escape the fire above them, they always surfaced into the flames that awaited them. Finally, no one in the water was alive anymore.

Where the cathedral had been was now only a pile of rubble. The Hotel du I'Independence and the surrounding buildings suffered in the same manner.

Father Roche watched the doomed city in its death throes. Then he heard another tremendous roar from Pelee and again another fireball emerged from the already smoking hole.

Just behind the second red flaming ball of fire, came black clouds rolling down the slopes in huge whorls. They mushroomed upwards then back down the slopes towards the burning city. One moment they would clutch at the ground, the next they would rise fifty metres before falling back to the ground again. The clouds of smoke reached the city and commenced to cross the city again with its red hot dust particles. The fireball seemed to him like it was living thing, glowing all the time, while from its centre, bursting explosions sent lightning-like scintillations high into the darkness. The original fireball rushed across the city again to meet its younger sibling. The two fireballs merged as one, and as such, they engulfed the entire city. The mulatto quarter was almost leveled to the ground. By now, few buildings remained standing anywhere in St. Pierre.

Andre motioned to Rachelle to climb onto the bed and stay in the cabin until he returned to her. On his way to the deck, he saw that many of the passengers had been already in their cabins. Some who had been asleep, were dead because they had left their portholes opened and were either poisoned by the poisonous gas in the pyroclastic flow or were drowned when the boat keeled over to both port and starboard and their cabins filled up instantly with water, trapping them like drowning rats.

When Andre reached the deck, he was aghast at what he saw. Blackened humans crawled about the deck, begging for water, some, when they reached the guard rails, climbed between the stanchions so that they could topple into the sea to end their agony.

He had no sooner been on the deck when the entire area was pelted with hot ashes. Then the ashes were followed by a rain of small hot stones, ranging in size from shotgun shot to pigeon's eggs. Most would drop into the water with a hissing sound but when some hit the deck, they did little damage to the structure as the decks had been covered earlier with a thick mantle of ash. After the stones, came a rain of hot mud and lava that was mixed with water, having the consistency of thin cement. Where it fell, it formed a coating over everything. The mud didn't seriously burn anyone but the steaming substance was quick to dry, thereby encasing everyone in a thin plaster-like cast.

Andre almost stumbled over a hideously burned figure in the deckhouse who feebly called out. "Please, would you get me some water? "

Andre told the figure that he would return with some water. When he finally returned to the deckhouse with a container of water, he brought Rachelle with him and when she saw the hideously blackened figure slowly moving about on the floor of deckhouse, she told Andre that she was going to pass out. He managed to convince her that it would serve no purpose.

The man continued begging Andre for water, but he knew they were too late. He died in less than a minute later with his arm reaching out towards the sea. They then searched for those victims who were still alive.

Meanwhile First Mate Ellery Scott had been blown down a hatch and soon became buried under carbonized corpses of seamen and crew members who failed to get down the hatch before they were incinerated by the superheated ash and blown down the hatch after him. Someone managed to pull him from the heap of bodies so he went forward to look for the Captain. He found him on the deck with one of the victims trying to help him get off his knees. He was terribly burned but despite that, his eyes weren't burned and he could see his first mate approaching him.

The captain asked, "What shape are we in, Mister Scott?"

"Pretty bad sir." replied the first mate. "I think we may be stuck in the mud. And we are on fire."

"Then you had better lower the lifeboats and abandon the boat."

"Very well, Sir. As soon as the lifeboats are lowered, I will come for you," said Scott who then went aft to get some of the crew to assist him.

Try as hard as they could, none of the lifeboats could be salvaged. They were either burning or the ropes holding them in the davits had burned through, thereby dropping the boats into the sea where they continued to burn. Scott went up forward to inform the Captain but all he saw was an empty forward part of the deck. He was to learn later that the captain had climbed to the edge of the boat and thrown himself into the sea. It was there that his agony ended.

Flames appeared to be coming from everywhere on the boat. The pumps wouldn't work as they were clogged with ash and mud so some of the crew lowered buckets into the water. A fire line was formed and the water was thrown onto the flames.

At about half past eight, the steamer *Roddam* steamed towards the *Roraima*. The boat was out of control. Scott attempted to wave it off but the boat edged towards the *Roraima*.

Many of the passengers and crew who were able to move about, went forward, believing that the *Roddam* was approaching their boat to rescue them. When it became apparent to them that there was going to be a collision between the two boats, there was a mad scramble to get to the other side of the boat. Several persons jumped overboard in a frantic effort to escape the collision.

Just as the two boats were about a hundred meters from each other, the *Roddam* veered off to port and just passed the *Roraima* by a few metres. The wash from the *Roddam* was enough to move the *Roraima* so as to drag its anchor from the mud.

The *Roddam* continued to steam away from the other boat and soon disappeared into the smoke as it headed out to sea. The *Roraima* now free from its former position in the harbour, slowly floated towards the flaming city.

Within the three minutes from the moment the initial fireball hit St. Pierre, the city had been completely destroyed. The waterfront was a mass of flaming wreckage. The mulatto quarter consisting of wooden houses burst into flames instantly when the fireball struck. The rest of the city was burning furiously but being of stone and concrete, it was mostly the interiors of the buildings that caught fire. Practically all the buildings had initially crumbled to the ground when the first blast came and the remaining buildings toppled to the ground during the second blast which was accompanied by an earthquake.

The Cathedral, the banks, the hospitals, the town hall, the theatre, the offices of 'Les Colonies', the military prison were all piles of rubble. It was as if the ruins had been there for thousands of years.

It was nine o'clock when Scott was able to take command of the burning *Roraima.* He ordered the distribution of lifebelts to everyone.

Scott went to find out what parts of the boat were aflame so he sent parties to various parts of the boat to locate the fires.

Andre left Rachelle to work with the wounded and dying victims and then he assisted the men in locating the fires on board.

He headed down to the cabins and saw smoke pouring out one of the cabins. He was able to kick the door in and as he did, the flames in the cabin shot out towards him. Inside the cabin were two bodies, blackened by the intense heat. Andrea reached in and closed the door again.

"Follow me!" yelled someone behind him.

He turned and followed the man who yelled to him. It was one of the boat's officers. Several of the other crew members were with him. They headed down the passageway and vanished into the smoke that was clogging the doorway. Andre stumbled over a body then saw one of the crew carrying a large four by four timber with him.

One of the cabins was burning furiously and, because of the heat, the lock in the door was jammed. The men smashed the timber through the door and as Andre had experienced before, the flames shot out of the opening.

Inside the cabin was a pile of mattresses which had been stored there. It took the crew ten minutes to douse the fire in the cabin and when it was done, Andre and the others went forward to the main hold. They fought their way through the smoke and suffocating atmosphere to reach another fire which was burning just a few yards from the entrance to the hold.

"We have to get this fire out immediately or the boat will blow up!" yelled the officer.

"Why?" asked Andre.

"Inside this hold," continued the officer, "we have three thousand cases of kerosene oil, a hundred large kegs of varnish and two hundred barrels of tar. And just above it, as you may have noticed when you were on deck, are ten thousand board feet of spruce lumber, enough to burn a city."

The men began to panic and one yelled, "Let's get out of here."

"No!" yelled the officer. "There is nowhere we can go if we abandon boat."

"That's right!" yelled Andre. "We must stay and fight the fire, or perish in the explosion that will follow, or drown in the sea."

Some of the men still paid no heed and ran down the passageway. The rest stayed behind.

The officer yelled, "Quickly! Some of you get buckets down here! Others of you form a fire line from this entrance."

The officer started pushing some of the men into the entrance to the passageway in which stairs headed up to the deck.

In less than ten minutes a fire line had been formed, with most of the survivors, passengers and crew on the boat working in the line. The buckets were passed down the hatchway from the main deck, to the passageway until they reached Andre and the officer.

Both men took turns tossing the water into the flaming storage room next to the main hold.

The officer turned to Andre and yelled, "We have to get into the main hold."

"Why?" asked Andre.

"Because, I suspect that the steel bulkhead between the main hold and the storage room may be red hot. If it is, then the combustion formed in the main hold from the kerosene and varnish may explode because of the additional heat from the bulkhead."

Andre and the officer opened the iron door, half expecting the hold to explode before them. Nothing happened. The two men went inside and one glance immediately told them that the officer was right.

The bulkhead next to the storage room was a dull red colour.

"Quick! Some of you hand us some of those buckets of water," demanded the officer.

Soon the two men were throwing water onto the red hot bulkhead. Steam shot back at them, almost scalding them. There was very little light in the main hold and what little light there was came from the flames shooting out in the passageway from the storage room.

"If we don't get the fire out soon, we will have to abandon the boat," yelled the officer.

"Yes I agree," replied Andre. "The flames in this hold aren't as bad as we suspected but if any of those flames in the passageway slip into the hold, it will ignite the fumes."

The officer then said, "I must return to the passageway to conduct the fight against the fire in the storage room. Will you stay in here and keep dousing the bulkhead with water?"

"Yes," replied Andre. "Just keep the water coming."

The officer left the hold and Andre could hear him bellowing out orders to the men in the passageway. Andre looked at the bulkhead. It was deep red in colour.

Andre was determined to get that bulkhead's colour back to normal again if it killed him. Which, as an after thought, dawned on him, "*It might at that.*"

Rachelle was meanwhile on the deck and was trying to care for the burned victims on deck. Many of the victims had been placed together. All about her were sailors, passengers, men, women and children, burned and dying, crying out feebly for water. When water was placed to their lips most of them couldn't drink the water because the flaming gases had burned their mouths and throats so terribly that in many cases the passages of their throats were almost closed. Many of them suffocated to death.

One man was crawling about the deck on his hands and knees seeking water. The man's tongue was literally burned out of his mouth. His body was burned black from his head to his feet.

The worse burns were internal. For some unexplainable reason the intense heat didn't initially penetrate the clothing but wherever the flesh was exposed it burned mercilessly.

Rachelle went over to a woman who was trying to comfort her three children, two boys and a little girl. The wretched woman's mouth could not be opened as her teeth were tightly closed. Rachelle took a small spoon and put some water on her lips so that she could sip it into her mouth. She died shortly after, unaware that her two boys had died just moments before her. Rachelle marveled at the way the woman bore the pain considering that she had been terribly burned.

By this time, the air was getting a little cleaner, therefore making it easier to breathe. A cool breeze began to blow from the sea, forcing the smoke to blow back inland.

The sun began to show itself through the diminishing dust clouds although smoke poured continuously out of the gaping hole in the side of and crater of Pelee.

Lava was also pouring out of the hole and down the slopes facing the city but Rachelle figured that it would be several hours before the lava stream reached St. Pierre.

In the city of Fort du France, Edward L'Heurre, the island's lieutenant governor, was waiting for news from St. Pierre. He had watched the smoke from the volcano soaring kilometres into the sky and knew from the series of explosions, that St. Pierre was going through its death throes. While he was in the governor's mansion, he wasn't sure whether he should act or wait for the news from Governor Mouttet.

"Sir!" exclaimed a clerk of the Governor. "There hasn't been any word from St. Pierre on the telegraph.

"Very well," remarked L'Heurre. "Follow me."

The two men left the mansion and headed towards the telegraph office.

"L'Heurre!" yelled out a voice.

The lieutenant governor recognized the voice of the editor of "Les Colonies."

"I thought you returned to St. Pierre last night." he said.

"Not likely." replied the editor.

"But you were so sure that the city was safe."

The editor said in reply, "I was until yesterday, then I realized that it was dangerous just being near St. Pierre. It looks like I was right."

L'Heurre nodded his head in the affirmative.

Chapter Twenty-two

The editor asked angrily. “Why didn’t you try to warn everyone?”

“I tried to convince the Governor but he said he would go to St. Pierre just to prove that the city wasn’t in danger.”

Another voice rang out and the lieutenant governor recognized the Captain of the warship *Suchet* walking towards him.

“Sir! continued the voice. “Do you have any orders for me?”

“Yes,” replied the Lieutenant Governor. “Get your boat over to the harbour at St. Pierre and see what you can do for them. Also stay there for more instructions from the Governor.”

“I doubt very much Sir, that he is alive. I believe that you are now the acting Governor.”

The lieutenant governor winced and replied. “I hope not.”

By the time he entered the telegraph office, reports of the holocaust began filtering in. Rumors were wide spread. The entire city was covered with ash. Part of the city had fallen into the sea. The volcano toppled onto St. Pierre. The rumor that seems to prevail the most was that a huge fireball had descended down the slopes of Pelee and burned the entire city and everyone in it. The lieutenant governor knew that soon the undersea cable would be destroyed so he sent a wire to Paris before that eventuality became a fact.

MAY 8TH 1902
TO MINISTER OF COLONIES. PARIS.
VOLCANO TOTALLY DESTROYED
CITY OF ST PIERRE AND BOATS IN
HARBOUR. PRESUME ALL THE

INHABATENTS AND GOVERNOR
ARE DEAD. WILL KEEP YOU
INFORMED.
L'HEURRE. ACTING GOVERNOR.
MARTINIQUE

Fernand Clerc, his family and a number of others on the Mount Parnasse were able to stand up finally and were shaking the ash off their clothes. For the past three quarters of an hour, they were lying on the ground for fear that the firestorm would sweep over the area where they were in. As it was, the fireball hit the mountain and glanced upwards, just missing the top of the mountain where Clerc and the others were. Fortunately the spot they had chosen was devoid of all plant life so no secondary fire ensued.

A number of the men in the outskirts of the town got together and decided that since the fires had died down a bit, with the exception of the mulatto quarter, they would re-enter the city in hopes of saving anyone that may still be alive. Clerc refused to go, saying the volcano might explode again. Slowly the other men descended the mountain.

No matter how much water Andre threw against the red hot bulkhead, it just didn't seem to do any good. The flames from inside the storage room just increased and it wasn't until nine o'clock in the morning that all attempts at putting out the fires were stopped. The reason for the useless battle against the flames in the storage room almost made Andre laugh hysterically. Apparently, several days earlier, one of the crew members placed several cases of temper lime, in the storage room to keep it away from the dampness that seem to be characteristic of all the boat's holds. Temper lime, a highly inflammable substance used in the making of sugar, burns when in contact with water.

The boat was doomed. There was no way that it could be saved. Scott ordered everyone to abandon boat but such an order was pointless. The four lifeboats were damaged and burned beyond repair.

The rescue party had reached one of the roads leading into St. Pierre. There was smoke everywhere but it was possible to see where they were going. The houses on both sides of the street were burning; many of them were just piles of burning rubble. The crackling fires up close and the roaring of the inferno in the mulatto quarter at the northern part of the city were the only sounds they could hear.

As they moved slowly down the street, they passed many bodies on the road. Almost all the bodies had no clothes on which in the minds of the men, meant that the victims had tried to flee their homes without getting dressed when the firestorm struck or their clothes had been burned off their bodies when they got outside.

The heat was still unbearable and the men shielded their faces from the raging fires that surrounded them.

The rescue party reached a small hill that overlooked most of the city. They could see that the area of destruction covered the entire city. The area of destruction, from the gaping hole in the volcano to the sea, covered an area of twelve square kilometers. Within that zone of destruction, life and vegetation and all man made things were gone. The destruction was absolute. The course of the tornadic blast was approximately six kilometers long and three kilometers wide. Where the course of the fiery blast had traveled across a narrow but high-walled valley, there were areas in which the fireball had passed overhead leaving the small houses still standing more or less erect. Unfortunately for the victims inside, all the available oxygen was sucked upwards to feed the fireball overhead. The victims gasped for breath but to no avail. By the time the small areas were replenished with more oxygen, the people had already suffocated to death.

The rescuers noticed that the hundreds of naked bodies on the outskirts of the city were face down and away from the volcano. To the rescuers it was obvious that the people had tried to flee the city without any hope of success.

It was about this time that Arnoux, the leader of the rescue party noticed a number of other people coming into the city to help. The second group was led by Father Roche. The two parties became one. That is with the exception of one of the members. She was a housewife who had been visiting a relative in Fort Du France and was just a kilometer outside St. Pierre when Pelee struck. She had run off, leaving the others, crying for her husband and children who were somewhere in the rubble of St. Pierre.

Father Roche noticed with horror that many of the bodies were split open with their innards hanging out. He realized that the intense heat had caused the bodies to inflate with the gases inside them, then burst. The smell permeated the area. It was a mixture of burning flesh, wood, cinders; a scorched putrid smell that gripped the throat and turned the stomach and sulfur from the gases that came from the fireball. Many of the rescuers were retching on the street.

In one place, two corpses were intertwined. It was difficult to determine the sexes of the bodies but it appeared as if one had been trying to shield the other. In one of the houses, a woman had fallen on her back, naked but very little of her was carbonized. One of her hands was on her breasts, digging into her flesh. The other seemed to be trying to protect her blackened face.

The rescuers stepped between the burned bodies that lay in the streets. When they reached Rue Victor Hugo, they saw the ruins of the Cathedral and the Hotel de L'Independence. It was clear to everyone that if the Governor and his wife had been in the Hotel or the Cathedral when the fireball struck, they would have perished. There were no walls standing of either of the two buildings.

Outside the smoking ruins of the Cathedral were hundreds of blackened bodies, many of them burst open from the heat of the two fireballs that crossed the city.

From Rue Victor Hugo the rescuers could now see the harbour because the area before it had been leveled. There were only five boats in sight, all of them afire. Seven others were at the bottom of the harbour. Two hundred men, women and children went down with them.

The rescue team continued along the Rue Victor Hugo which was a pile of concrete and boulders. Around the Place Bertin rose tier after tier of rubble. Not a roof remained. Any of the walls that still remained just rose a few metres from the ground.

The further they went into the city, the more complete the destruction was. When they reached the mulatto quarter, they turned back. The way was blocked by corpses everywhere, distended by gasses and charred.

The fires in the mulatto quarter were still burning furiously. There was no point in attempting to rescue anyone in that inferno so the rescuers headed back towards the centre of town.

When they reached the Jardin des Plantes, a noise was heard.

"Listen!" yelled Father Roche.

"What did you hear?" asked one of the men.

"I think I heard a moaning voice," the priest replied. "There it is again."

The other men heard it and when they reached the park, they saw the woman who searched for her family talking to a blackened man crawling on his hands and knees in a small puddle of water.

"It's probably her husband." said one of the men.

Father Roche approached the woman and looked at the burned man. On closer examination it proved not to be the woman's husband. It was Professor Landes. He was hideously burned. His face was one huge blister; his eyes had been seared from their sockets. His hair was burned away.

"Pelee." gasped the professor.

"What are you trying to say?" asked the woman.

The professor made no reply but went limp and died. The rescuers turned and left the blackened corpse. He would not speak of Pelee again. It was just past nine thirty in the morning.

"No one," sobbed one of the men.

"What?" asked another.

"No one is left alive," replied the first.

When the professor died at nine-thirty, the rescuers began to head out of the city. His death was the last for the city of thirty thousand inhabitants and refugees. The rescuers knew that the entire city had been wiped out. Not a man, woman or child had survived. Still, some decided to search the outer fringes of the city in hopes that some survivors may have lived through the holocaust. They didn't believe they would find any but there was a chance. They looked helplessly at the military prison as they passed it on their way to the outskirts of the city. It was a pile of smoking rubble.

On board the *Roraima*, panic was everywhere. There was no hope for those who could not swim. They knew that the boat was going to explode in a few minutes. A raft of sorts had been built on the boat but it wouldn't hold very many. When it was dropped over the side, some crew and passengers jumped into the sea and swam towards the raft. This was their assurance of getting a place of the raft.

Others remained on board the boat to help the dying.

Andre and Rachelle were giving water to a moaning figure when Scott pulled at Rachelle.

"Come, my dear," said Scott rather sadly. "There isn't anything you can do for him now. The boat is going to explode."

"But we can't leave him like this," cried Rachelle.

"We must or we will die. It is an easier death coming for him when the boat blows than if he continues to live like that."

Andre and Rachelle and the first mate lowered themselves down ropes hanging from the main deck to the sea below. When they reached the water, they could feel the strong current pulling them under. Normally the placid water wouldn't have a current, but somehow Pelee had caused this strange phenomemen. They swam towards the raft which was drifting away from the boat.

Behind them were twenty or thirty dead bodies with perhaps a few who might have just been barely alive.

Suddenly a tremendous explosion was heard from behind them. They turned around in the water and looked at the boat. It was about a hundred meters away. A huge flame, bright orange in colour, shot out of the main deck. The flame mushroomed a hundred meters into the sky. The heat became unbearable so to escape it, the three of them dove under the water. Andre could see the red glow even while submerged. When they came up for air, the flames were billowing over them. Again they submerged underwater.

Then another tremendous explosion was heard while they were under the water. They could feel the terrific impact as the shock waves pounded the water at their bodies. When Andre and the others came to the surface they saw pieces of lumber coming down all around them. Again they submerged but by the time they resurfaced again, the boat was sinking. In a few moments, the burning boat slid below the surface of the water. Another great explosion rocked the area underwater and again they felt the impact against their bodies.

Andre, Rachelle and Scott swam towards the raft. They were pulled onto it, and then they looked about them. There were pieces of debris all around them. On the raft were only twenty-four persons, many of them badly burned.

The *Suchet* steamed into the area and rescued the survivors of the *Roraima* from the raft.

In the late afternoon, Andre and Rachelle were transferred to one of the boats in the harbour of Fort Du France. The sun was just beginning to set in the west when the boat they were on began to steam out of the harbour and sail northwest.

Andre and Rachelle stood on the deck of the boat and stared at the smoking city of St. Pierre as it slowly slipped below the horizon. Then they watched the smoking volcano slowly follow suit. By the time the sun had disappeared and darkness had encompassed the area, all that could be seen was a slight reddish glow just over the horizon, the source of the glow reflecting the fury of the volcano onto the clouds above it.

Andre and Rachelle talked of their plans for their future. Behind them, Rachelle had left her home, family and friends in the doomed city. She knew that her family and friends had gone to the cathedral to pray and that they, like the city, had died praying to God. As the cool breezes of the night brushed against her face, she felt the warmth of Andre's body as he pressed his close to hers. She and he would share a new life together and as time passed, the pain of her loss would slip away in the same manner that the light from the volcano was gradually slipping away from them.

Seven years later, Andre and Rachelle took their six-year-old son Michael to see the Barnum and Bailey Circus that was performing in Paris. It was while they were visiting that circus, that Andre met the only survivor that had lived through the holocaust in St. Pierre. It was none other than the condemned prisoner, Louis Auguste Ciparis whom Andre had visited while he was in St. Pierre. After the show, Ciparis talked with Andre and told him that he survived because his cell had been completely sealed from the outside because of the ash build-up. He was partly burned nevertheless, but his worst injuries came from the huge blocks of stone that crashed into his cell. He was to suffer three days trapped in his cell before searchers accidentally found him under the rubble. He was taken to Morne Rouge where Father Mary nursed him back to health again.

He smiled at Andre when he then said, "A surprised government in Paris suspended my sentence and I am finishing out my remaining years as an exhibit with the Barnum and Bailey Circus." He laughed when he then said, " I guess I am a living testament that even the bad can be spared by God and given a second chance by Man.

Andre began thinking about the old soothsayer who forewarned him that the woman he truly loved was doomed. Was she thinking of Monique? Andre decided that it would be better for him and Rachelle if he simply disregarded that aspect of the old woman's premonition because over the years, he began to believe that the woman he truly loved was really the mother of his six-year-old son. He knew, fate has a strange way of changing the lives of everyone so it follows, he thought, that it can change a premonition also.